This Is Not About Love

By USA Today Bestselling Author
Carissa Ann Lynch

This Is Not About Love

Limitless Publishing, LLC
Kailua, HI 96734
www.limitlesspublishing.com

Formatting: Limitless Publishing

ISBN-13: 978-1-64034-229-3
ISBN-10: 1-64034-229-X

Dedication

To all my loyal readers and to my sister—for believing in me before I did.

Chapter One

Making pancakes at one in the morning made Violet Cromwell feel like a single woman again. Breakfast on a whim was exactly something she would have done when she lived alone in her cozy, little townhouse in Williamsburg. Smiling to herself, she scooped the thick batter into a measuring cup and poured a perfectly cylindrical cake into the butter-lined skillet. As the batter began to sizzle with a low hiss, she retrieved a small plate and eating utensils from the cabinet drawer. The drawer squeaked loudly as she closed it with her hip, and her bare feet produced a familiar creak as she pattered across the wooden floor. The house seemed quieter when she was alone, and the creaks and groans were a welcomed and reassuring companion in the three-story turn of the century house. Some people hate the upkeep and past associated with an old home, but she had to admit that she loved this place much more than the boxy one-bedroom townhouse with its whitewashed walls and cookie cutter designs.

Violet slapped the pancake on her plate, poured a glass of milk, and set out butter and syrup on the small, oak dining table in the eat-in area of her kitchen. She settled down into one of the stiff, rose-backed chairs and sipped her milk as she imagined what it would be like to be here all alone, every day, for the rest of her life. She could get a cat, and they would share TV dinners in the great room…ugh. Maybe being single was not such a grand idea after all. She needed more than a cat and a lovely, old house. Perhaps the real problem was not that she preferred being alone, but that she preferred solitude to living with Alex. She shook her head in disgust and tried to push guilty thoughts out of her mind as she stuffed a syrupy bite of pancake into her mouth. She had suddenly lost her appetite, which seemed to be happening a lot lately.

The fact of the matter was that Violet was anything but single. She had been married for only a year now, and as of two months ago, she had even acquired a boyfriend. *Is that what I'm calling him now?* she questioned herself. She laughed aloud as she thought about the mess she was in, nearly choking on the half chewed food in her mouth. She swallowed hard, but the laughter quickly turned to labored breathing, and she scooted her chair back, dizzily anticipating another panic attack. The panic attacks were also becoming a usual occurrence.

She took several deep breaths and tucked her knees up to her chest like she always did when she was nervous. It was a habit that began when she was a young girl—pulling her knees up to her chin and wrapping her arms around her legs in order to fit in her small wardrobe closet when her father was on a drunken rampage. She buried her face into her upper thighs and took a ragged breath. *I'm not a little girl anymore*, she reminded herself, and concentrated on her breathing for several more seconds until she felt her heart rate go down and her breathing steady. The panic attacks had started when Michael Sinclair entered her life and turned everything upside down. Oh, who was she kidding? Her life was a mess before he came, but Michael was the catalyst for wanting to make a change. She never should have married Alex. Her mistake hung over her like an ominous cloud, threatening to burst from within at any moment and produce a real downpour of problems.

Everything about Violet and Alex's relationship had been rushed. They bought a house and moved in together after only two months of dating, and he proposed on their one-year anniversary. Less than three months after his proposal they were married, and only three months after that, he had taken a job that required him to work out of state for months at a time. So, she had basically been living on her own since their wedding day.

His decision to work out of town would not be so bad if she actually missed him. Being alone again made her realize how independent she really was, and all that she'd been missing for the past year and a half. All of a sudden, she had friends again, and even the movies she watched and the meals she ate were changing back to what they used to be. The day that he left to work out of town, her heart ached for the so-called "honeymoon period" they would miss, but then her life quickly resumed, and she was surprisingly content with having the house and so much time to herself.

None of her decisions were about *we* anymore, only *me*. The fact that she didn't miss him confused the hell out of her. But what confused her even more was that he didn't seem to mind being away from her, either. His nightly calls came less and less, and the last few times she'd called his company hotel room, he'd been "out with colleagues," according to the receptionist. The whole purpose of taking the out-of-town position was to increase their income, but after nearly five months of working, he'd sent very little money. The one time she questioned him about the money, he'd given her an angry response about the high costs of eating out and gasoline, and then accused her of being ungrateful. Violet was not a money-hungry female, and it wasn't like she needed his income to survive; she simply wanted an explanation as to why she'd given up her husband for this out-of-state job that seemed to be producing less than half of the income he'd made before.

When he forgot her birthday, and refused to come home for her grandmother's funeral, she started feeling a lot of resentment and suspicion. She was usually the kind of girl that stayed at home with a good book and took a hot bath on a Saturday night, but two months ago she'd agreed to go out for drinks with some of her female colleagues, and that was the night everything changed.

After about five drinks too many, she'd decided to hail a cab and head home, but when Michael

Sinclair stepped out of that cab, she somehow knew she wasn't going anywhere anytime soon.

It was not her first encounter with Michael Sinclair. In fact, she knew that gorgeous face all too well. They had grown up down the street from each other for most of their childhood. However, Michael was six years older and attended an all-male, private school in a neighboring town. In the spring and summer, she would ride her bike past his large, family home peeking up at the attic window that faced the street, hoping to catch a glimpse of his raven-colored hair, emerald green eyes, and his golden tan. Occasionally, she'd see him sliding open the old window to his room and climbing out on the roof for a smoke. One time he even caught her staring and waved, causing her to hit the brakes and fly over her handlebars. Like a knight in shining armor, he glided down the sloping roof, nearly tumbling to the ground and skinning his perfectly tanned knees in the process. He rushed to her side and picked her up off the pavement. He carried her to his front wraparound porch, mysteriously darted inside, and then returned with a first-aid kit. He knelt down on the porch and very softly placed a Looney Toons Band-Aid on her scraped-up knee. If only he had known how long she'd kept that old crusty Band-Aid in her ballerina box...

After "The Rescue," Michael Sinclair had been the muse for every dreamy fantasy she'd had as a girl. In fact, she'd relived the day of her ludicrous bike wreck a million times in her mind—only she improvised the real events of that day with cheesy alternative endings—Michael kissing her, then carrying her into his house and up the spiral, rickety staircase to an old, romantic canopied bed.

That night at the bar, seeing him step out of that cab, brought back butterflies she had long since forgotten. When he stepped out of the cab, he looked right at her, or right through her, she'd thought to herself with disappointment. She had looked away as people often do when they recognize someone they either don't want to see or don't feel comfortable enough to address, and she lamely started digging through her Coach purse as though she had lost something of great importance. Then she felt a touch on her elbow, and there he was, all six feet of him, staring down at her five foot self with a smile that could melt even the coldest heart.

"Violet Cromwell?"

She flashed her most confident smile, but her shyness was difficult to conceal even to a complete stranger. "Michael Sinclair," she said with no hint of a question in her voice. "It's good to see you. It's been so long…" *My instinctual ability to make polite, small-talk sounds extraordinarily lame*, she thought. Or then again, maybe the quiver in her voice was a result of a few drinks too many and the excitement of seeing him again after all these years. She laughed nervously. "Are you here to rescue me again?" The moment felt surreal and she regretted how drunk she sounded. Perhaps he didn't even remember "The Rescue." His silent, questioning stare did nothing to soothe her nerves. Then suddenly he reached forward and embraced her. He smelled of Guinness.

"Violet, you are so beautiful. It must be fate that I ran into you, because I've never forgotten the way you looked on that unicorn bike. I wanted to kiss you that day on my porch, but you were so young and I was…stupid…and a little scared. I always hoped we'd run into each other someday, and now here you are right in front of me!"

Michael looked her up and down approvingly, and she let out a breath noisily as she finally remembered to breathe. "Me too," she responded shyly, lowering her chin to her chest and glancing down at her feet. She fixated on an ugly crack in the pavement, her eyes following it until she noticed a scuff on his shoe. He reached out and lifted her chin slowly until she could no longer avert her eyes from his. His hand felt rough but good. And those eyes…they were as green as she remembered. Michael Sinclair was apparently one of those men that just got better with age, because the boyish features she loved so much had evolved into manly exquisiteness. His black hair was sprinkled with little flecks of gray. She couldn't recall ever having the nerve to look this long or hard at him. Maybe she'd hit her head on the dance floor or passed out in the back of her co-worker Lisa's Suburban and this was some sort of black-out fantasy/dream. But it wasn't a dream—at least not the kind of dream you wake up from.

Their reunion outside the bar had spiraled into hours of conversation and even longer hours of feverish lovemaking in her canopied bed. *If only we could have stayed in bed forever*, she thought as she stood up and tossed the pancake in the garbage and placed her plate and fork in the sink. Instead, they had woken up to reality and, unfortunately, they were both attached to other people and had acted on impulse. However, neither regretted it, and as he gathered his keys and wallet on his way out the door that next morning, he had told her he loved her and promised to call soon. He kept good on his promise.

Violet and Michael had seen each other at least a dozen times since then, but they had not yet ventured back into bed. They'd met for lunch on several occasions, and a few times they just sat in his old truck listening to music and making out like young, high school kids in random parking lots.

To complicate things further, Michael had a fifteen-year old son named Elijah, and before his current relationship, he had also had a wife. He had full custody of his son and was in a serious relationship with a new woman who had a fourteen-year-old daughter whom he had grown seriously attached to. Recently, he and said woman had bought a house and become engaged. Violet loved him with every ounce of her body and always had. She knew she didn't want to be alone in this big house; she wanted to be with Michael. But a relationship with Michael, a real relationship, was impossible right now because he was spoken for— not to mention her own husband and commitments.

Violet climbed the steps to the third-floor attic, which she had recently converted into an additional bedroom. The bedroom was where Dr. Middleton, the founder of her town and original owner of the house, had slept, so it felt right to use the room for more than just storage as Alex had suggested. She stripped off her thin, pink camisole and crawled under the large duvet wearing only her panties. The silky duvet felt good on her skin and reminded her of Michael's touch. She hadn't washed the sheets since that night, and she could still vaguely smell his cologne...or so she thought. Whether real or imagined, it smelled superb. In only one week Alex would be back for a whole month. She shuddered at the thought of facing him and sleeping next to him instead of Michael. She wondered what the hell she was going to do as she drifted off to sleep.

Chapter Two

"Like I said before...I want her in the front. She's pretty enough to be up front, and she's better than Suzie and all those other girls, anyway!"

Penelope Pinkerton was not the kind of woman that liked taking no for an answer, but Coach Elly Anderson didn't like being told how to run her cheerleading squad. Penelope had grown up with a silver spoon in her mouth, so to speak, and she demanded the best for herself and her daughter. In addition, she was one of those moms that liked to live vicariously through their daughters in the hopes that they would be younger, more successful versions of themselves.

"Ms. Pinkerton, I understand your frustration, but she's only been on the team for a few months, and some of these girls have been waiting for a front spot for years. She's only a freshman, and she still has a lot of work and maturing to do," Coach Anderson tried to explain.

Penelope nodded and flashed an insincere smile as she gathered up her daughter's gym bag and her own Gucci handbag. "I'm sorry, Coach Anderson. I used to cheer myself, you know, and I guess I'm letting my own competitiveness go to my head. I only want what's best for Angie, and I'm not sure if she told you or not, but she was captain of her squad at her old school."

"I assure you she's doing fabulous, and I always look out for the girls' best interests. She seems to be enjoying herself, and we can't forget that's what is most important here," Coach Anderson reminded her gently. She lightly patted Penelope's arm and offered her a reassuring smile.

Angela Pinkerton skipped over to her mother and coach, grinning from ear to ear.

"Mom, did you see that? I nailed my back tuck this time—without a spotter!" Angela exclaimed.

"Of course I saw, Honey, wonderful job!"

Angela waved to Coach Anderson and thanked her for another grueling practice. "See you tomorrow, girls!" she waved back to her fellow squad members as she followed her mother out of the gym.

Penelope handed the gym bag to her, and they locked arms as they strolled out the exit doors of the gym and headed across the parking lot to their Cadillac Escalade.

"Hey, jerk," Angela greeted her soon-to-be stepbrother.

He was slumped down in the backseat, and as usual he was lost in the land of Nintendo DS. He finished whatever it was he was doing and looked up at her with a sheepish smile. "You're the jerk, jerk," he said, shoving the game system into his

11

ratty, old Land's End backpack and buckling his seatbelt. "How was practice? Did you learn how to curl your hair and paint your nails today or what?"

She punched him in the arm and scooted over next to him, reaching for her own seatbelt. "As a matter of fact, jerk, I actually landed my back tuck today without a spotter. So there," she taunted, sticking out her tongue at him.

***

Elijah Sinclair couldn't help but smile at Angie. She was the most gorgeous girl at Riverside High School. Unlike some of the other pretty girls, she wasn't a snob. She was smart and friendly and seemingly unaware of her own beauty. She was technically the "new girl," but needless to say, she was having no problems fitting in with everyone. It was hard not to love Angie with her bubbling personality, contagious smile, and natural good looks.

When Elijah's father introduced him to his new girlfriend, Penelope, he was less than pleased. His mother had run off several years earlier, and he kind of liked having his dad all to himself—not to mention that Penelope seemed like a snooty bitch with all her jewelry, fancy clothes, and an endless assortment of bizarre looking purses that apparently cost a small fortune. She was nothing like his mother, but hell, maybe that was a good thing too. However, he still hated the idea of his dad and Penelope together.

But Elijah's mind quickly changed when she

introduced him to her daughter, Angela. Angie was the prettiest girl he'd ever seen, and she was nothing like her prissy mother. Plus, he and Angie had a lot in common. He played basketball at Riverside High School, and she was a cheerleader at Crimson. His mom had pretty much abandoned him at the age of six, and her father had died when she was young. Plus, they both loved to joke around and play video games in their spare time. Needless to say, they hit it off from the start.

Elijah had mixed feelings about his father's engagement and the subsequent new home they had decided to purchase together as a family. Living together meant Angie would transfer to Riverside, and he would get to see her all the time. That was a good thing. But now that his dad and her mom were engaged, didn't that make them like brother and sister? He shuddered at the thought as he refrained from looking over at her long, tan legs and golden blonde hair.

After the engagement, they had purchased a monstrous home that was so not his dad's style in a ritzy, new building development. The development was located in the small town of Oaksdale, which was where his father had grown up. Every house in the subdivision looked identical, which sort of gave Elijah the creeps. The fact that his father apparently loved Penelope was probably the only reason he agreed to give up their comfortable man-pad. The inside of the new house was awesome though, he had to admit, and he and Angie practically had the entire second floor to themselves. He was also relieved that the move didn't mean changing schools, since they were still located within the allowed school district for Riverside. Angie was okay with switching from Crimson to Riverside High because Riverside had the best cheerleading squad in the state. So, all in all, the whole transition seemed to be working out for everyone—except for the whole weird brother-sister thing.

***

Penelope started the SUV and slowly pulled out of the school parking lot on to the main street. Oaksdale was a small town that consisted of six cross streets and a main road. Penelope had lived in Mellville, a much larger neighboring town, most of her life. *Moving here was worth it though*, she thought. Oaksdale did not consist of much, but it had one thing going for it: Michael Sinclair. She would have moved anywhere with him no matter how small or big. They'd been dating for only a short time but soon they would be married, and they had recently bought a brand new home in Oaksdale's most prestigious neighborhood, Glenn Heights. Oaksdale had been Michael's choice so she had insisted on choosing the house. She had chosen the biggest and best house in town.

It was the kind of home she had always dreamed of with its clubhouse, gym membership, and perfectly manicured lawns. She felt like a princess, and Michael was her prince. Elijah needed a mother, and Angie needed a father. It all seemed to be working out perfectly, really. And the kids seemed to get along so well.

She adjusted her rearview mirror so she could see them in the back of the SUV. "Elijah, you ready for pizza?" she asked.

"Hell yeah we are," Angie answered for him.

"Language, Angie," she scolded, raising her eyebrows in the mirror.

"Yes, Mom…" Angie rolled her eyes, giving Elijah a conspiratorial wink.

Elijah leaned forward. "Can we stop for ice cream too?"

"I can do even better than that. Your dad got you a cake and ice cream. He's meeting us at the pizza place," Penelope told him.

"How did he get off so early today?" Elijah asked.

"He took the day off…said he wouldn't miss your sixteenth birthday for the world."

***

Elijah smiled and glanced out the window as they passed Mandy's Fruit Market and old Dr. Middleton's house on the hill. His eyes glazed over, and for the first time in a long time, his thoughts drifted to his mother. Did she know it was his birthday? If so, did she even care? He pushed the thoughts of her aside as he so often did as they pulled into the pizza place. His father's Jeep Cherokee was already there. He hopped out before the car had even come to a full stop and ran over to greet his dad.

***

Angie reached for her door too, but Penelope reached back to stop her, lightly placing her hand on her leg, "Try not to overeat, honey. You know how those extra calories can slow you down in the gym. And you need to fit in that skirt for the game next week," Penelope reminded her.

"Okay, Mom," Angie whined as she looked achingly out the window at Elijah and Michael. She wished her mother accepted her as easily as Michael did Elijah. It was hard to imagine that he would be her stepfather soon. Even though she liked him well enough, she yearned for her own father. Her memories of him were vivid despite how young she was when he died. She remembered that he was tall with kind eyes and a smile that could light up her whole world. Then, one day, he was gone. A sudden, massive heart attack, her mother had explained. To an eight-year-old, losing a parent was the end of the world. Her own heart had been literally ripped from her chest—at least that's how it had felt for many years after his death.

Her father was a gentle, carefree man who had brought out the very best in her mother. At least that's how she remembered it when she allowed her mind to drift back into her hazy, eight-year-old memories. She missed her father dearly, and she knew he would never get on her for her weight or any other petty, little thing like her mother always did.

As she watched father and son embrace, she felt slightly ashamed for feeling sorry for herself. Elijah had lost a parent too. In a way, she was luckier than he. At least her father hadn't abandoned her by choice. His mother had apparently checked out early for reasons unknown. She walked up to her soon-to-be brother and slipped her hand into his. "Let's go pig out, birthday boy…"

Penelope and Michael followed behind them. "I'm glad you took the day off. He's so excited, Michael," Penelope said.

"It was worth it. God knows he deserves a real birthday. The last two years I've had to work on his birthdays," Michael admitted with a tight frown.

"Well, not anymore," Penelope replied. "He has a whole family to celebrate with now."

Michael nodded and opened the door to the restaurant for her. He seemed to have a lot on his mind, but everyone else was too happy to notice.

Chapter Three

Lexi Ambrose kicked the Malibu's tire with her black combat boot and hollered an angry string of curses at no one in particular. This is just great, she thought as she leaned on the hood of the car and pulled a cigarette out of her army-green satchel. She reached for the lighter in her jacket pocket but then realized she'd left it beside the bathroom mirror at home. "Damn it!" she hollered.

She opened the car door and yanked her duffel bag out onto the sidewalk. Carrying this thing is going to be a bitch, she thought. She swung it and the satchel over her right shoulder and limped up the street toward work. Luckily, she'd gotten a flat only two blocks from work. God knew she couldn't afford to be late again today…

Lexi finally saw the pink neon sign of the Clamshell buzzing in the soft moonlight. She waved to the guard, Charlie, as she trudged through the front door.

"Working up quite a sweat already, eh?" Charlie teased. She shot him a look that said don't fuck with me and wiped her brow as she slid the bags off her arm onto the floor of her *office*. After digging a pack of matches out of an old jacket that hung on her chair, she lit up a cigarette and took a deep, relieving drag.

It was Friday, and although that meant she would probably make good money today, she hated Fridays. There is nothing more depressing than spending a Friday night seducing men you would never want to go home with. And this particular Friday was worse because it was the second of April, and that meant it was Elijah's birthday.

Lexi stubbed out the cigarette and quickly started powdering her face, neck, and arms. She ran a comb through her long, dark hair and put on red lipstick. One of her *colleagues* took a seat at the dressing table next to her and gave her a curt nod. The girls here were less than friendly, but Lexi supposed that's how it was at most strip joints. She used a Kleenex to blot her lips and then gave herself a smile that was intended to be reassuring but looked sinister instead. Showtime!

Chapter Four

Violet's body felt stiff and achy as she made her way down the second flight of stairs to the great room. She headed straight for the kitchen, the way she did most mornings, and started a pot of coffee. Her night had been restless and riddled with strange dreams that she could not even begin to recall at this early hour.

She reached for her cigarette pack and headed into the great room. She threw a few logs on the fire and settled down on the brown leather sofa under her favorite afghan. This was her favorite room in the whole house, and it was her routine to start her mornings out right here, just like this. She lit a cigarette and leaned back with her eyes closed. Alex would be home in two days. He'd called last night to give her his flight information, and although she offered to pick him up from the airport, he'd strangely insisted upon taking a cab and meeting her at home. She had mixed feelings about his return, and she had been busying herself with housework and shopping all week in preparation of his arrival.

She planned on making enchiladas on his first night home since they were his favorite. "What am I doing?" she groaned aloud, "this is all so crazy." The doorbell chimed in response, and she nearly dropped her cigarette in her lap. Who the hell was at her door this early in the morning?

Expecting a nosy neighbor, or worse, some annoying salesperson, she pulled open the door with a sigh. To say she was surprised to see Michael Sinclair on her doorstep was an understatement. She looked at him in confusion, since they had both agreed not to meet at her home after their first irresponsible rendezvous. But his warm eyes melted her heart, and she moaned with delight as he grabbed her around the waist and carried her into the great room. He sat her down on the couch and pressed his lips to hers. His lips felt great, like they belonged there all the time. "So, to what do I owe this pleasure? I thought we agreed…" she started to say.

He shushed her by placing a finger to her lips. Kneeling on the Oriental rug, he pressed his face in her lap, and she stroked his hair. They sat in silence for several minutes before she asked him if he was okay "Talk to me, Michael," she pleaded.

He looked at her with wet eyes and said, "I've missed you, terribly, and I just don't know what to do with all of these feelings I have for you…"

It was her turn to shush him. She led him into the kitchen and pulled out a chair for him before heading over to the coffee pot. She poured him a cup and lit another cigarette for herself before settling down on the chair beside him.

"I feel the same way, Michael. I can't sleep, I can't eat...hell, I've been having panic attacks for weeks now," she admitted. He shook his head in regret and buried his face in his hands.

"I'm so sorry, love. I feel like such a shithead." His eyes filled with tears again, and she placed her hand over his gently.

"Michael, this is just as much my fault as it is yours. For God's sake, you are the one with children in this situation, so that makes me the homewrecker here," she said with a look of disgust and shame on her face. "I've never cheated on anyone, and I've never dated someone who was engaged, let alone someone with children," she said.

"Me neither...well, we can't say that anymore because here we are," he reminded her.

"Michael..."

"Yes?"

"Maybe it's best that we don't see each other anymore. I mean, I wish we would have gotten together when we were young, or before I got married and you got engaged, but we didn't. I mean, the truth of the matter is, I don't know what I'm going to say or do when Alex gets home. I may just confess the second he walks through the door, who knows? I'm a horrible liar, and I don't even know if I can go forward with this marriage regardless of whether you're in the picture or not. Everything has changed now. Everything..." she said as she stared out the old picture window, focusing on her vegetable garden instead of looking at him.

She wanted to cry. She could remember the day that she and Alex had planted the seeds for it. It was a delightful day, and filled with much excitement, as they read the directions and information on the packets and then coaxed the tiny seeds into the dirt with loving care. They had fantasized about how big their vegetables would grow someday—ten foot tall corn stalks and heads of cabbage the size of bowling balls. From here, she could make out the shape of several potatoes, tomatoes, and corn stalks. *Our garden is flourishing, and like everything else in our relationship, Alex is going to miss it,* she thought. He had been gone so long that his absence had become the norm; it was when he was home that the house felt unusual and unfamiliar to her.

Michael reached for her hand again, but she barely noticed. All she wanted to do right now was crawl into her bed, listen to depressing music, and cry alone with her head under the pillow. Michael wiped her tears away and the next thing she knew, he was lifting her out of the chair and carrying her up the steps.

"But Michael..." she started to protest. Who was she kidding? If they were going to end it, she at least wanted to make love to him one last time. Who could blame her?

Michael carried her up the first flight of stairs, but he started to struggle on the second flight, and the next thing she knew, they were both bursting with laughter. He sat her down on the top landing and reached for his lower back.

"You were lighter when you were eleven," he joked. She promptly kicked him in the shin and took off running toward the large canopy bed in the center of the attic floor. She plunged onto the cushiony bedspread face first, burying her face into the satiny duvet. She heard him undressing, and then she felt him slipping off her sweatpants. She was embarrassed by his confidence, yet reassured and turned on by his amazing ability to take charge in bed. She had had few lovers, and none of them came close in comparison to Michael.

He removed her panties and rolled her over before pulling off her t-shirt and sports bra. He looked at her body appreciatively, and surprised by her own boldness, she laid back on the bed, placing her hands behind her head. She enjoyed letting him look at her, and she was reminded of how different her relationship with Michael was to her relationship with Alex.

It wasn't that Alex was bad in bed; it was just that she and Michael seemed to take sex and intimacy to a whole new level. He made her feel like a model, and sex came so naturally she didn't even have to think about—or worry about—any of her usual insecurities the way she did with most men. Michael made her feel sexier than she had ever felt before, and she loved it.

After making love, they lay on the bed naked and smoked Romeo and Juliet cigars. Apparently, Michael had taken the day off to spend with her, unbeknownst to his wife. He wanted to see her again and couldn't wait, he'd explained.

"You just wanted to bang me again," she joked, and they giggled like old pals. He puffed on his cigar, and she did the same.

"I can't believe you bought this old place, Violet. It's just the way I remember it as a kid...Did you know that I was friends with Dr. Middleton's son, Lucas?" he asked.

"No, I did not know that," she said, propping herself up on her elbow so she could look into his eyes as he spoke.

"Yeah, we were pretty close for a while before I left for college. I stayed the night here a few times, and Lucas held some pretty cool parties here back in the day."

"Wow, that's weird. I never knew him. I guess he went to Riverside High with you?"

"Yep. Sure did. I think he moved to Arizona or somewhere like that."

"I'm surprised old Dr. Middleton didn't leave this place to him then," Violet pondered. "You would think that he would want his son to inherit an old family home such as this."

Michael chuckled. "I'm not surprised. Don't you remember the old man? He was an ass…"

"Still, you would think he would want his son to have it instead of some stranger. I guess I just assumed he had no family, and that's why the house went up for sale after he passed away."

"Well, Lucas was basically his only family. And from what I remember, they didn't get along well at all. Lucas couldn't wait to get the hell out of town, and I think the old man was glad to see him go off to college. If I recall correctly, I think the old man was pissed that his only son didn't want to be a doctor. I think he wanted to be an architect, and the old man fought the idea until he finally pushed him away for good. My guess is that when Lucas left town, that was the last time they saw each other. All

I know is I'm glad you got this old place. It's cool as hell, really, and much better than my cookie cutter house in Glenn Heights."

The mention of his house brought Violet back to reality. He was supposed to be getting married. He had a son and a stepdaughter, and most importantly, he had his fiancée, Penelope. Violet relit her cigar and rolled back over on her back. She stared up at the vaulted roof of the attic and admired its intricate design.

"Why are you here, Michael? Why are you so unhappy with your life?" she asked, keeping her eyes fixed on the ceiling above.

He didn't answer right away, and in truth, Violet wasn't sure she wanted to hear his answer.

Then suddenly, he began to talk—not about his current fiancée—but about his marriage to Elijah's mother and how it broke his heart when she left. It was obvious that he had loved her. He described the way they met at a bus stop in Reno. He had decided to travel and see the country before embarking to college, but within a week's time he had met Lexi, and he was ready to stop and stay wherever she was. According to Michael, she was scrounging for loose change in the dirt near the bus stop, desperately trying to come up with enough funds to catch the next ride out of there. From Michael's vantage point, she looked like a homeless woman with her back hunched over and dirt in her nails. When he handed her some change, she was startled and looked up, and that's when he saw the beautiful contours of her face, and he realized she was not your run-of-the-mill homeless girl.

She was younger than he, about Violet's age, in fact. She was practically an orphan, he explained. Her parents were drug addicts, and she had been taking care of herself since she was a pre-teen. Despite her rough upbringing, she was sweet and idealistic about her future. Lexi wanted to be a famous dancer someday, but most of all, she wanted to be a mother.

"To make up for her own mother's shortcomings, I presume," Violet interrupted.

Michael replied, "Perhaps. Lexi followed me to college," he went on. "We were inseparable, and in many ways, our relationship was too passionate."

"Explain," Violet encouraged him.

"Well, I hate to say this, and I hope this doesn't offend you, but my relationship with Lexi reminds me of our relationship in a way: passionate and sweet, but painful at the same time," he said.

Violet raised her eyebrows.

"Lexi was into drugs and sex. She was a great girl, but when she partied, man, she really partied. And it wasn't just her, it was me too. I mean, hell, we lived in a little apartment down the road from a college campus. It was party central, so to speak."

Violet nodded. She loved hearing Michael talk about his life, and she wanted to know everything, but the look in his eyes was a reminder that he had an entire life before he knew her, and she definitely wasn't the first woman he had ever adored.

"Then she got pregnant. And the partying stopped. Well, at least I thought it had, but I have always suspected that she still used some during her pregnancy. When Elijah was born, Lexi was so

27

happy, and so was I. We were young, but we were determined to do it and to be better parents than our own." He paused, and Violet left him to his own thoughts as she imagined the whole scenario. Michael stood up and started pulling on his pants and boots with a pained look in his eye. "But we were not any better. In fact, we were inherently worse, because she left when he was six, and I did nothing to stop it from happening," he said with a crack in his voice.

Violet stood up and embraced him. He sunk his head into her bosom, and she stroked his hair with her fingers. She didn't know what to say, so she just held on to him, speaking soft words of encouragement.

The next thing she knew, he was tearing off her pants again, and they were falling back into bed together. *So much for ending this thing tonight,* she thought as she arched her back and moaned with delight as he caressed her thighs and kissed her breasts.

"I'm so sorry about what happened, Michael," she whispered. "It must have been so hard for you and Elijah…"

For the second time that day, she allowed him to shush her. "I am in love with you, Violet," he whispered into her hair. "I have pined over you since we were kids, and I will be damned if I am going to let another woman walk out of my life without telling her how I feel and not trying to stop it. So, please just shut up and let me love you tonight."

So, that is exactly what she did. They made love

until the sun went down, and then she fell asleep in his arms; she dreamt of nothing, as there was no need. Her dream was lying right beside her.

Chapter Five

Penelope stirred the fried potatoes and glanced out the kitchen window into the darkness of the night. The driveway remained empty. *Where the hell is he?* she wondered, looking down at her Rolex. It was nearly eight thirty, and even on his busiest nights, Michael was usually home no later than eight. She had prolonged dinner for him, and the kids were getting antsy for their meal as they hovered around her in the kitchen.

"All right, fine. I'm taking up supper," she said, letting out a deep sigh.

"Yes!" Angie whooped. Tonight they were having her favorite meal, which consisted of hamburgers, fried potatoes, and macaroni and cheese.

Angie took a seat next to Elijah at the dining room table as her mother placed two plates in front of them. She carried over silverware, napkins, and two glasses of Sprite. "Mmmm...looks good, Penelope," Elijah said.

"Thank you," Penelope replied. She was

distracted, and Elijah and Angie both knew it. They shot each other knowing glances as Penelope stomped into her bedroom, closing the door.

Penelope sat on the edge of her four-poster bed and dialed Michael's cell phone number for the hundredth time that day. It wasn't unusual for him to have it off, since he really wasn't supposed to use it at work, but considering the fact that he was late, she thought he would have at least called her by now to tell her he'd be late for supper. She tried the number one more time and decided to give up when she heard his familiar voicemail once again.

"I'm taking a bath," she called out to the kids, heading into the spacious, four-fixture bathroom that was adjacent to her bedroom. She locked the door behind her and stripped off her nurse's uniform and undergarments. She let the water run as she inspected herself in one of the his and hers wash basin mirrors. She couldn't help but think how tired she looked. She pulled her hair into a high ponytail and inspected the growth between her eyebrows. *It is definitely time for another wax*, she decided.

The water was ready, so she stepped in slowly, allowing her body temperature time to adjust. She lowered herself into the tub and let out a relieving sigh as she leaned back against the pillow cushion that she had recently added to the backside of the tub.

Closing her eyes, she tried to listen for Michael at the front door, hoping he'd come in, see her stretched out like this, and get instantly turned on. But there was no Michael, and after giving her face a good scrub and spraying off with the showerhead quickly, she decided to get out and check to see if he was home yet. She wrapped a towel around her waist and used another towel to twist up her hair.

"Bedtime, kiddos!" she hollered out to them as she headed back to the bedroom to get changed. She stuck her head out the door once more. "I mean it! It's a school night!" The tone in her voice must have made the message clear because she heard the Xbox and TV go off within seconds, and then they stomped up the stairs to their second-story bedrooms. Penelope put on shorts and a lacy camisole before heading out into the living room to wait for Michael. Where the hell was he?

The living room opened up into the kitchen, and she once again walked over to the front window. It was nearly ten o'clock, and she had to admit that she was becoming less angry and more worried by the minute. Michael was always so timely, and it just did not seem like him to be so late without calling. At quarter after ten, she'd made up her mind. She used her iPhone to dial his work number and tapped her foot impatiently as she was placed on hold.

Michael worked for a shipping company, and they held late hours, but working this late was very atypical for Michael. She rarely called his work number. In fact, she couldn't even think of a time that she had called it before. But she was worried, and Michael would understand that. She just wanted to make sure he hadn't had an accident at work and if he had left hours ago, then maybe he had been in a car wreck on the way home...she didn't like thinking such grim thoughts.

"B and J Shipping," a young, peppy girl announced, "how may I help you?"

Penelope told her who she was and asked if Michael had gotten off work yet. Yet again, she was placed on hold, but Miss Peppy quickly returned on the line, only she no longer sounded so peppy anymore.

"Ms. Sinclair? Are you still there?" Peppy asked.

"Yes, I am," Penelope answered, unable to hide the irritation in her voice any longer.

"He's not on the schedule today..." Peppy revealed hesitantly.

Penelope paused briefly, then thanked Peppy and started to hang up before another thought crossed her mind. "Miss? Can you tell me if he will be in tomorrow? Silly me! I forgot that he told me he was taking some time off this week, and I've been out of town planning our wedding, so we haven't talked much this week...I'm due back in town tomorrow so if he's off, I thought I might surprise him," Penelope said.

The receptionist gave out a sigh of relief, as though she hadn't revealed too much information about her boss's whereabouts after all. "Yes, he's off all week," she informed her.

Penelope thanked her again and hung up.

She was stunned and her eyes welled up with tears. What was going on? Why would Michael take a week off from work and not tell her? Sure, he had been off for Elijah's birthday, but he told her that he had the day off, not an entire week.

So, then, she wondered...if he's not at work, and he's not at home, then where else could he be? She poured herself a glass of Chardonnay and tried to carry it to the bedroom, but her hands were too shaky. She sat down at the dining room table but left her drink untouched.

Michael had been distant for the past couple of months, but she had just chalked that up to a busy workload and stress with the move and wedding plans and all. Now that she really thought about it, they hadn't had sex in nearly two weeks. *What if*...no, she wasn't going to think thoughts like that. Surely, when Michael got home, he would explain all of this. Hell, maybe he took the day off so he could go buy her an engagement present or make plans for their honeymoon? After all, Michael did love surprises.

Speak of the devil, she thought, as headlights glared through the shiny, glass kitchen window. She ran to the bathroom to hide her tear-stained face. She locked the door and re-started the bath water just as he turned his key in the front door lock. She pressed her back against the door and realized she was foolishly holding her breath. The knock on the bathroom door startled her. She turned off the faucet and called out, "Honey, is that you? I was worried!"

For a moment he was silent, but then he responded through the door, "I'm sorry, Babe. I lost my cell phone in the truck, and they worked me like a dog today. We have some new clients in town this week, so I will probably work late tomorrow and Friday too."

She plopped down on the edge of the tub and wrung her hands nervously. She was stunned.

"Honey? You okay in there?" he asked.

She called out, "Yes, I'm fine—just washing my hair. That sucks about your new clients. I hate when you have to work late."

"Yeah, me too. Well, I'm going to undress and hop into bed. I am totally beat," he replied softly through the door.

"Good night. I'll be in in a little while," she answered back. She stared blankly at the bathroom tiles and even went so far as to count them. Her bathroom consisted of eighty-six tiles.

Penelope felt numb. Meeting Michael was the best thing that had happened to her and Angie in a long time. He had a good job; he was great with the kids, and he was ridiculously handsome. She knew he had a past and a little bit of a wild side, but surely, he wasn't cheating on her, was he?

Regardless of what he was doing, it was only a matter of time before she would discover the truth for herself. *Nancy Drew* was her favorite book series as a child, and after tonight's revelations, it seemed as though it was time to do a little detective work of her own.

Chapter Six

Until she could get her tire fixed, Lexi was stuck riding the bus. She dug some loose change out from the bottom of her satchel and handed it to the bus driver, then headed for a seat in the back. Riding the bus was not her favorite pastime. For one, it stank of urine and body odor. Two, it was filled with passengers who either talked too much or gave her the creeps. Last but not least, buses reminded her of Reno, and Reno was the last thing she wanted to think about.

Lexi was scheduled to be at work at seven. As long as the bus stayed on schedule, she would make it just in time. Billy, the owner of the Clamshell, was intolerant of tardiness, and Lexi had definitely had her fair share of tardiness since she had started working there last year.

Stripping was not her idea of a good job, but without a degree or high school diploma, she didn't have a lot to offer prospective employers. Reggie, her sometimes boyfriend, had taken her to the Clamshell one night with some of his buddies. She didn't mind strip clubs and didn't protest when they suggested she tag along with them one drunken evening as they prepared to go. Not only did she not mind strip clubs, but she actually viewed the men as the ones being degraded, not the women. If men want to throw their money away just to look at something they'll never get, and could easily get from their wives at home, then that makes them pathetic, not the girls.

That night at the Clamshell she was offered a job. After months of searching for employment and being on the verge of losing her apartment, she accepted the position and had started the very next day. The truth was, despite her liberal views on strip clubs, she hated working there, and she did, in fact, feel pretty degraded by it.

The bus screeched to a halt and several passengers started heading up to the front. This was not her stop. She stared out the window at the city with its strip malls and small specialty shops lining the streets. One of the shops was called "Unique Gifts for the Child in All of Us." Lexi stared at the model airplane that was displayed in the front store window, and she thought about Elijah. His first word was *mama*, and his second word was *plane*. She smiled sadly at the memory. Even as he grew older, he still loved airplanes, and when he was five he'd built his first model airplane with Michael by his side helping him. She remembered how full of love she had felt that day—for both her husband and child.

Lexi looked away from the store window and then looked back again. "Driver, wait!" she called out suddenly, surprising herself and jarring awake the woman beside her who had been snoring softly. "This is my stop," she said as she climbed over her neighbor's lap and pushed her way to the front.

As the bus pulled off, she stood on the sidewalk staring at the airplane that she pretty much had just given up her job for.

"Fuck it," she said aloud and reached for a cigarette. She wanted to buy it for Elijah, and she had enough cash in her pocket. *Screw the tire*, she thought as she tossed the lit cigarette to the ground and then jogged across the street. For the first time in a long time, she felt excited about something.

Chapter Seven

Violet leaned back in the computer chair and stretched her arms up over her head. She needed a break. She had spent the entire morning and half of the afternoon cleaning the house again in preparation of Alex's arrival, and then the rest of the day she had been working on volume eight of the *Manolo's Secret* series that she had been writing for six long years now. When she wrote her first book, there was no way she had ever dreamed it would really get published. But after her book proposal was rejected by nearly three dozen agents, Christopher Fontaine had come to her rescue. He had started out as a small-time agent, but over the years, he had become quite a success, and "It all started with you!" he liked to remind her from time to time. Christopher had worked his ass off to find a publisher willing to take a chance on a first time author. But in the long run, his diligent work had paid off, and now here she was, working on book eight of a successful series that had recently hit the bestseller's list. She couldn't help but feel proud of what she had accomplished, and even though she had enough money to leave her part-time job at the library, she loved her co-workers and couldn't imagine giving up her position there anytime soon. Books were an integral part of her life, and there was rarely a time she could ever remember a day going by without reading or writing.

Violet loved writing and reading books more than anything. She grew up poor, and one of the greatest highlights of her life was taking weekly trips to the library with her grandmother. Her mother had died in a car crash when she was a baby, and her father was too busy getting drunk to take care of her half the time, so Granny Alice was the closest thing to a parent she had.

Granny Alice did not have much, but she treated what she did have as though it were gold. She lived in a one-bedroom, shotgun house in the middle of a dead-end street, three doors down from Michael's parents' gorgeous, old Victorian home. Granny's house stood out like a sore thumb with its minute size and rickety paneling, but she was not the kind of woman who concerned herself with others' perceptions; since childhood, she had encouraged Violet to worry only about her own self-image. "We may all look different on the outside, Violet, but if you lift the skin and peek underneath, we're all the same. So, never think that you're better, Violet. And most certainly do not ever think that you're worse," she would say over and over again; it was always like she was telling her the first time.

Every Saturday, Granny took Violet to the library to check out a new book. Some of Violet's greatest memories were of sitting on the porch, drinking iced tea, and reading aloud to her grandmother. "You read marvelously, Violet," she would always say. "Please tell me what happens next."

Violet would sit there and read all day if Granny would let her. It wasn't until she became older that she asked Granny why she didn't read herself. That day, Violet was shocked to discover that her grandmother had never learned to read. From that day forward, she was determined to teach her grandmother how to read, and she would never forget the way her grandmother's eyes lit up with enormous pride when she checked out her very own book at the library. Violet remembered the day just like it was yesterday, and her chest felt tight as she remembered saying, "You read marvelously, Granny. Please tell me what happens next."

Violet saved her work and shut down the computer. Writing had been difficult lately. With all the newfound drama in her life, one would think she could sit and write for days, but that wasn't the case. Christopher had been calling daily to inquire about her progress on the book, and she had been dodging his calls left and right. She was nowhere near done, and she didn't feel like hearing him bitch.

Violet headed up to the second floor and stared at the bed she shared with Alex. He wouldn't be pleased when he found out she had converted his storage area in the attic into a spare bedroom. But then she realized it was silly to worry about getting upset over a bedroom when what he really needed to be angry about was the new man that had been occupying the bed itself.

The curtains were drawn, and she decided to open them to let in some natural light. It was a lovely day, and here she was cooped up in this old, creepy house. As old and creepy as it was, she knew she would live here forever. She had adored this place since she was a little girl. Granny and Violet used to pass by it every Sunday on their way to church, and sometimes they would stop and park across the street on their way home just so they could look up the hill and admire the old place. Violet knew her grandmother loved Dr. Middleton's house, probably because her tiny little house was such the polar opposite of a grand place like that. She vowed to buy it for her grandmother one day, but Granny had been dead for nearly eight years now—a deadly combination of Alzheimer's and lung cancer.

"I hope you're here with me, Granny," Violet whispered. For some reason, that thought cheered her up. She changed her shoes and decided to head into town.

Alex would be home tomorrow, and today she was meeting Michael at the Filmont Inn. *It seems rather tacky and cliché to meet at a hotel, but so is having an affair with a married man,* she thought. Earlier in the week she had received a cryptic message in her inbox; it was an odd reminder for a "business date" with Michael Sinclair at the Filmont Inn. Violet did not respond to the strange message, as she suspected Michael sent it written in such a way that if his wife examined his inbox, their plans would seem nothing more than a casual work encounter. Violet had decided to go ahead and meet him. She couldn't help but want to spend the night with him despite her better judgment, since it was the last night they would have an opportunity to do so before Alex returned.

Violet had made another decision of her own. After tonight, she was going to tell Michael she wanted him to be happy, and if that meant losing him, then she would just have to accept it. She had decided she needed to cut him off and make a go at her own marriage while he figured out what he wanted to do about his own engagement and current predicament. After hearing his story the other night, she realized the importance of their actions. She never wanted to cause him the kind of pain he had endured from his first wife, and who was she to stand in the way of Elijah having a stepmother and family he so deserved?

If Michael wanted to leave Penelope, then he would have to do it for his own reasons, and the same went for her and Alex's marriage. If it was meant to be, then they would be together again in the future. More than ever, she was certain her love for Michael was above and beyond anything she had ever felt for another human being. She was more than happy just loving him from a distance if it meant never having to see him cry or hurt the way he had the other night.

Violet locked the back door and squeezed behind the wheel of her Geo Tracker. She wanted something special to wear tonight when she met him at the hotel. It had been so long since she had purchased anything new for herself, and she felt almost giddy as she slowly descended the hill and headed into town. Even though tonight was going to be bittersweet, she could not wait to see Michael again. She wanted simply to rest her head upon his chest, enjoying the warmth of his body and silkiness of the hair on his chest. Even when they were apart, she felt so sure about her love for him. *I must be crazy*, she thought. *No man has ever made me act this lovesick and girly before, but Michael Sinclair just has a way with the ladies, I suppose.* She smiled.

In town, she selected a sleek, black dress with lacy trim and low neckline. She also chose a flimsy negligee to conceal underneath the dress and a racy pair of black kitten heels. It had been so long since she had last indulged in a shopping spree, but she had never felt so sexy or alive, and everything she slipped on seemed to somehow fit so perfectly today. The entire day seemed perfect, and she was antsy with excitement about her evening plans with Michael. She stepped out of the store and into the sunlight. It was gorgeous today, and Violet felt certain that nothing could spoil the day ahead.

Chapter Eight

Penelope used her hip to close the heavy Escalade door, waved to her neighbor, Joan, and headed up the front walk to their home in Glenn Heights. She dug around for her keys, but her purse was so deep, and it was full of makeup and other random accessories. She plopped down on her front porch swing, and angrily began dumping its contents at her feet all over the concrete patio. Joan gave her a funny glance and then turned back to her gardening.

"Nosy bitch," Penelope muttered under her breath. "Ah ha!" She eagerly grabbed a ring of keys. She scooped up her mess, tossed it back in the bag, and let herself inside. Penelope had left work at noon. She loved her job as a nurse, and there were few people in life more important to her than her clients. Furthermore, she really could not afford to take the time off today, but she had to; there was work to do. Detective work, that is…

Penelope dropped her heavy bag on the tiled entrance floor and did a quick walk-through just to make sure Michael wasn't home. He had "gone to work" again this morning. She had been tempted to just jump in the car to follow him this morning, but she had to get the kids ready for school, and she'd had to go into the hospital for a few hours to finish up some overdue paperwork—not to mention the fact that, unlike Michael, she could not run around all day because she had to be home to take care of the kids after work. She felt angry as hell as she thought about the fact that she was pretty much taking care of Angie and Elijah all on her own while he was out running around doing God knows what.

After chugging some caffeine, Penelope made her way into the bedroom. She started opening drawers and looking through everything. She didn't know what she was looking for...some sort of clue...maybe some definitive sign he was having an affair or living some secret life that required him to take mysterious days off from work?

Her first instinct was to forage through the contents of Michael's desktop computer. With the way of the world these days, and its many technologies, a man can easily have an affair via the Internet. Penelope was not naïve, and she even, in fact, knew the password he used for his email. She loaded the computer and accessed his inbox, scrolling down desperately through its contents, looking for anything that seemed personal in nature or otherwise suspicious. There were a few short messages between Michael and his secretary, but nothing that gave Penelope cause for concern. There was, however, a recent message sent to a woman named Violet Cromwell, and her name was unfamiliar to Penelope. However, B & J Shipping was an enormous enterprise, and there was no way she could know everybody he associated with at work. The content of the message to this Violet person was regarding a luncheon at the Filmont Inn, and it was also not uncommon for Michael to meet potential clients at hotels or local convention centers. Penelope sighed, shutting down the computer, and began searching her and Michael's bedroom erratically.

The bedroom produced no results. Other than the living room, kitchen, the kids' bedrooms, and the three bathrooms, she was left with only one other idea of where something might be hidden, although she wasn't sure what that something she was looking for might even be.

Penelope had never been out to Michael's storage shed, but she knew where he kept a spare key. She dug around in his dresser drawer until she finally felt the small, metal key with her fingertips. She tucked it in her pocket, and after checking again to make sure no one had pulled in the driveway, she headed out back to the shed.

She undid the padlock, yanked open the shed door, and quickly slid inside, closing the door behind her. She felt around in the dark for the pull chain light and was relieved when she finally found it. Penelope hated the dark.

Her eyes adjusted to the light, and she was disappointed to see that it was only a quarter of the way full, mostly with Michael's tools and lawn care equipment. There did not appear to be anything suspicious, but just as she was turning to leave, she spotted a cardboard shoebox on a top, wooden shelf. Climbing was not her strong suit, so she went back inside the house to retrieve a step stool. She climbed up on the stool and slowly edged the box down from the shelf with her fingertips. Michael must have put it there, because God knows she and the kids weren't tall enough to store something that high.

The box was small and light enough to tuck under her arm as she hurriedly darted back inside the house. For some reason, she didn't want Michael to come home and find her snooping through his stuff. She couldn't imagine him getting angry about it, especially since she had every right to be pissed off and suspicious after the stunt he pulled, lying to her about being at work. But the thought of being so desperate embarrassed her. She tried to picture her mother rummaging through her father's things, but the thought only made her laugh. Her mother would not think twice about snooping around; she would have wacked her dad with a frying pan and confronted him about his lie directly instead.

Penelope pried the top off the box and pulled out what appeared to be a stack of tattered letters and pictures. The pictures were of Michael, Elijah, and Lexi. Penelope had seen a picture of Lexi before, but she had thought most of them were gone. Michael told her that he couldn't stand having them around anymore after she left, so he finally put them all away and eventually tossed them out with the garbage. Just one more lie to add to the growing list, she thought warily.

Penelope flipped through the pictures and could not help but feel jealous. Lexi was exquisitely beautiful. Even though Michael and Elijah rarely spoke of her, Penelope just knew what women always know: that Lexi had been the one, at least at some point in time for Michael.

Penelope opened one of the letters and was appalled to see that it too, was from Lexi. After opening the other letters she realized that they were all from Lexi—love letters, apparently. She tossed the box across the room with an angry grunt just as she heard a knock on the door. "Crap!" she cried, tossing the contents back into the box and hiding it under the sink.

Penelope straightened her hair and smoothed out the wrinkles in her work uniform as she made her way to the front door. It was the UPS man. *Hmmm*, she thought, *maybe Michael has been busy ordering me some sort of gift*. She opened the door and gave the UPS man a welcome smile.

"Package for Elijah Sinclair," he announced as he handed her the board to sign with her electronic signature.

"What is it?" she asked, signing her name as *Penelope Sinclair* instead of using her maiden name.

"You know how many times a day I hear that question, lady?" he asked with a smile. "I have no idea. I just deliver the packages."

He handed her a medium-sized, brown box addressed to Elijah with his and Michael's previous address on the package. Apparently, whoever had sent it was unaware of their new address, but UPS had been kind enough to look up their forwarding address.

She carried the box inside and set it on the table. Without a second thought, she started pulling off the heavy tape. She knew it was wrong not to wait for Elijah, but after the recent discoveries she had made with Michael, she couldn't help herself. Who would be sending sixteen-year-old Elijah a package? According to Michael, they had no close relatives that they kept in touch with. She got her answer as she opened the box to find a white piece of paper taped to the outside of a model airplane kit. The paper simply read:

"Happy Birthday. Love, Mom."

Penelope was taken aback. After ten years, she suddenly decides to send Elijah a gift? Penelope wondered incredulously. Suddenly, she had a thought. Was Michael seeing Lexi again? Was she back in town? Is this why he was skipping work and running around behind her back? Why the hell would she just send something out of the blue if she hadn't talked to Michael or Elijah in nearly a decade!

Penelope sat down on the living room couch and decided to send Michael a text. She had to get to the bottom of this and quickly. Both her and Angie's happiness depended on it, and she was not about to let Michael make a fool out of her! What would her mother think when she found out?

Her worried thoughts were spinning out of control as she texted Michael and clicked the send button. She texted him that she was getting off work early and asked if he wanted to meet for lunch.

Penelope groaned loudly as she received his response.

Michael: *I'm too busy today, Sweetheart...sorry...I probably won't be in until supper late 2nite so plz don't wait up.*

Penelope knew what she had to do now, and it was not going to be pretty. It was time for a good, old-fashioned stakeout. Nancy Drew would be so proud!

Chapter Nine

Lexi woke up from a nightmare covered in sweat. She was relieved to be awake even though she couldn't really remember what the dream was about. Something about loud music blaring in her eyes while some gross, old man hovered over her...no, not a man, she remembered, but some sort of beastly creature...

She laughed at herself and rolled over to look at the alarm clock. She had been having bad nightmares for years now, but the one she had last night was most certainly a direct result of the everyday trauma that she had to endure at the Clamshell. The club definitely had its fair share of beastly, old men and loud, blaring music.

The alarm clock told her it was three in the afternoon. *How the hell did I sleep so long?* she wondered. She hopped out of bed and headed straight for the shower just as she did most mornings. She stopped in the hallway to listen for sounds of Reggie, but concluded he must have stayed at his own place last night, or he crashed at one of his friend's houses.

Lexi bent over the sink and brushed her teeth. Her muscles ached, and she felt grimy from sweating so much in her sleep. She washed the toothpaste out of her mouth and took a quick shower. She strolled out of the bathroom naked and was startled when Reggie turned the corner. "Damn, Reggie! You scared the hell out of me!" she grumbled. She headed past him so she could put on some clothes, but he grabbed her arm, and he grabbed it hard. "What the hell!" she hollered.

But this wasn't the first time Reggie had put his hands on her, and she knew why he was mad.

After purchasing the present for Elijah the other day and overnighting it to him, she had been so happy that she had treated herself to a hotel room at the Carlton. That night she had wanted to celebrate alone in a place that felt clean and new and offered great room service. For one night only, she wanted to feel like a queen and forget all about her shabby, one-bedroom apartment and her crappy job.

Apparently, Reggie did not want an explanation. He just wanted to punish her with his fists. The first blow was expected, and she did her best to block it, but he just aimed lower with his other fist. He caught her on her right side with his fist, and she hit the ground, gulping for air.

"Where have you been, Lexi?" he asked, though it was not really a question. He kicked her in the side again with a worn-out, brown boot. It hurt, and this time she rolled over on her back in pain and put her hands up pleading with him to stop.

But her pleading only seemed to agitate him

more, and this time he landed a kick to the side of her head. For a moment, all she saw was blackness...then she opened her eyes and slowly pulled herself to her knees and started crawling to the bedroom.

"I waited all night for you, bitch! I even went to the club trying to find your slutty ass, but Billy said you never showed up!" he yelled.

Surely, the neighbors will call the police this time, she thought groggily as she continued to crawl away from him. But the next thing she knew, Reggie was sitting on her back, pinning her arms above her head. She jerked her legs wildly, but it was no use. "Reggie..." she tried to plead, but her voice cracked, and she imagined how good a glass of water would taste right now.

He grabbed her hair and pulled her head back at a painfully awkward angle. "What's that, bitch? What are you trying to say?" he hollered into her left ear.

Lexi tried to find her voice again, but the next thing she knew he was beating her in the head with his fists, and then the blackness enveloped her, and she didn't open her eyes this time.

Chapter Ten

Penelope parked her Escalade on the side of a deserted road and grabbed the siphoning hose that she had borrowed from her neighbor, Tootsie Daniels. She glanced up and down the street for cars, and it appeared as though the coast was clear. She started siphoning the gasoline out of her car into a rusty old gas can she'd found in the shed. She had read how to siphon gas online, but it was not as easy as it sounded.

However, after a while she got the hang of it, and when she was finished, she felt oddly proud of herself for figuring it out all on her own. She placed the evidence of wrongdoing in the trunk and slid back in behind the wheel. She made it approximately two miles before the car began to sputter. "Showtime!" she squealed with delight. She pulled the car over to the side of the road and pulled out her Blackberry.

Her mood blackened as she realized she was cheering herself on for tricking her fiancé. There was nothing about this situation worth cheering about. She covered her face with her hands, and for the first time in days, she didn't try to stop the tears. She felt awful. Her fiancé was sneaking around, and she was sneaking around in order to find out what he was sneaking around about. *How ludicrous!* she thought. How can I get married to a man whom I barely even know or trust? Why are we keeping secrets from each other already? Isn't that what people who have been married forever do when they suddenly get bored with each other?

Penelope let out a loud sigh in exasperation. She had to go forward with her plan, and in order to do that, she had to send a text to Michael. She took her time typing out the text, and reread it a few times to make sure it didn't sound fishy. *I ran out of gas!* she reminded herself. *There is nothing fishy about running out of gas*, she thought with a sigh. She hesitated for a moment longer and then pressed the send button.

Penelope had chosen this road purposefully for two reasons. One, it contained very little traffic, and in fact, she had not even seen one vehicle so far. Two, it was only a couple of miles from Michael's workplace, so he had no excuse not to come to the rescue of his soon-to-be wife no matter how busy he was at work—*not to mention the fact that he's not even really at work*, Penelope thought, and she was filled with disgust and anger.

She glanced down at her phone, eagerly awaiting his response and growing more nervous by the minute. What if he really did have his phone off today? It's not like she could call B & J Shipping, considering the fact that he really wasn't there. Was she going to have to walk two miles to get gas on her own?

She groaned at the thought. "That would be just my luck. Drain out my own gasoline in the hopes of getting rescued, only to discover that the only person who can rescue me is myself," she muttered under her breath.

Penelope was relieved when she heard the familiar beep of her Blackberry. It was Michael! His text read that he was on the way.

Forty minutes later, he showed up with a plastic gas can in tow. Penelope had covered up her tear-stained face with another coat of concealer, and she brushed her long, blonde hair. She was going for the whole "damsel in distress" look. But Michael paid her no mind. He went right to work filling up the tank with gas, and he seemed irritated when she explained she had gone into town and forgotten to look at the gas gauge. Michael once again appeared to be distracted by something, and he could barely look her in the eye.

"All done," he said. He screwed the cap back on the gas can and headed to the back of the car, presumably to place the empty can in the trunk. "No wait!" Penelope cried out, "I don't want the gas to leak out onto my shopping bags. Will you put it in the backseat?" she asked. He did as she requested and leaned forward to give her a quick peck on the cheek.

"Michael?"

"Yes?"

"Are you okay?"

"I'm fine, dear, just overwhelmed with these new

clients of mine at work," he responded, finally looking into her eyes for longer than three seconds. He paused for a second, as though he wanted to say more, but then he just patted her arm and told her he had to get back to work.

Penelope watched him pull away. She felt certain something was going on, and after the package Elijah received this afternoon, she was convinced it had something to do with Lexi Ambrose.

She started the car and pulled out behind Michael. She followed him to the stop sign. She watched him go left, and then she turned right. After driving for several blocks, she pulled into a church parking lot and turned around. The whole point of this charade was that she wanted to tail Michael and see what he was up to. But now she just felt so damned depressed that she considered going back home. She could hear her mother's voice very clearly in her head as she instructed her at an early age to, "Never chase after a man, Penelope!" According to her mother, Jeanie, no man was worth chasing.

"If he's not chasing you, then go find a man who will," Penelope reminded herself aloud. Even her voice was starting to sound like her mother's, and that scared her. Her mother's advice on love obviously didn't work for herself because Penelope's father had finally left her five years ago, and her mother lived alone with a cat and seldom dated anyone. She seemed shrewd and miserable, and Penelope didn't want to be either of those two things.

Penelope picked up speed and hurried to catch

up with Michael. After all, he was the man she loved and wanted to marry. She was willing to chase him around if it meant getting to the bottom of this mystery.

Chapter Eleven

The hotel room at the Filmont Inn was extraordinary. Violet had arrived an hour earlier with her new heels in tow and had been happily surprised to find a room filled with daisies (her favorite), chocolate-covered pecans (also her favorite), and champagne. As soon as she arrived, she kicked off her tennis shoes and jumped on the bed.

Jumping on the bed was a ritual that she and Granny had started when she was young. Anytime they went to a nice hotel, which was not very often because Granny couldn't afford it, they would both try out the bed first thing. Trying out the bed meant estimating its softness by seeing how close they could get to the ceiling when they bounced on it. After she concluded that the bed was indeed pretty soft, she poured a glass of champagne and hungrily ate three pecans. She decided it was time to check out the bathroom facilities, and she carried her champagne and an unlit cigarette in with her. The bathtub was like a Jacuzzi, and there were two his and hers sinks lined with tons of soap, shampoo, and toiletries.

Michael had errands to run, and he had encouraged her to go to the hotel whenever she liked and check herself in. She was thankful to have some time to relax and get ready before his arrival.

Violet started her bath water and sat on the toilet, lighting her cigarette. She felt great. Michael would be here in two hours, and that gave her just enough time to take a long, hot bath before slipping into her new lingerie, dress, and heels. She'd bought a curling iron at the boutique also because she wanted to fix her hair for once.

Violet peeled off her clothes and examined her naked body in the full-length mirror on the back of the bathroom door. Even with her hair tossed up in a loose bun and no makeup, she had to admit that she looked pretty good. She felt like she was glowing, and she knew it had to be because she was truly in love.

She took down her bun and let her long, dark locks fall to her shoulders. Her eyes were bright blue, and according to most people, they were her best feature. She was short and stocky, but her curves were in all the right places. Granny used to tell her that she was naturally beautiful without even trying. Maybe the champagne was going to her head, or maybe it was love, but for the first time, she actually saw what her grandmother was talking about. She did have natural beauty, and although she had always been insecure about her height and small, curvaceous figure, today she liked what she saw in the mirror. She could not wait for Michael to see her tonight too.

Chapter Twelve

Penelope was beginning to feel rather foolish. She had been following Michael at a safe distance for hours now, and although he definitely wasn't at work, as he had earlier claimed to be, he wasn't doing anything too suspicious either.

After filling up his Jeep Cherokee with gas, he'd driven to a local restaurant for lunch. At first, she wondered if he was meeting up with someone, but after watching him through the restaurant window from across the street for nearly an hour, she decided that he was doing just what it appeared: eating lunch. He finished his shake, paid his bill, and then drove to a barbershop. Unless he was gay, she didn't think he was cheating on her in a barbershop. She chewed on her nails for nearly an hour waiting for him to come out. She nearly fell asleep waiting, but perked up just in time to see him walk out, sporting a new haircut and shave.

Michael was so handsome, and she felt so guilty for following him that she was half tempted to just pull up next to him and end this whole charade.

Most likely, he just wanted some time to himself...just like I do occasionally, she scolded herself.

But instead of turning around and driving back home to get the kids off the bus, Penelope decided to finish what she had started. Michael's next two stops were the post office and dry cleaners. "This is getting boring…" she complained. After he exited the dry cleaners with two clean suits in hand, she was about to give up. But somehow she had a gut feeling that she hadn't seen all there was to see yet.

Michael's next destination was a gas station, and since there were limited areas where she could hide her vehicle, Penelope drove on up to the Filmont Inn and parked her car in the back where she still had a good view of the nearby gas station. Michael went into the store and returned with two paper sacks. "Wow, Penelope! You managed to catch your husband running errands today on his day off. Whoopee!" she exclaimed sarcastically and slumped down in her seat. Boy, did she feel pretty stupid—not to mention pathetic, paranoid, and psychotic!

Michael turned right out of the gas station and right in the direction of where she was parked at the Filmont Inn. Originally, she had planned to pull out after him as he passed, but at this point it was almost eight o'clock, and he was probably heading home from *work*. She needed to go home. *The kids were probably starving to death and rotting their brains with that damned Xbox*, she thought, shaking her head.

But just when she was starting to feel better, her

whole world came crashing down. Michael was turning into the hotel where she was parked! Had he seen her?

Apparently he hadn't, and his reason for coming to the Filmont Inn had nothing to do with her, since he parked his Jeep and headed inside, carrying his two suits and his two paper bags.

Penelope imagined herself jumping out of the vehicle and confronting him right then and there in the parking lot. She wanted to smack him across the face and then throw her engagement ring on the ground. But in reality, she stayed in the car. She was too shocked to move yet, and her stomach was twisting and turning as she realized that there was no way Michael was up to anything good. *It's Lexi*, she thought. *That careless bitch is back in town, and she's lured him here to try and win him back.* But then she remembered the email from earlier, the one about a business meeting at the Filmont Inn with a woman named Violet. Was the name Violet merely a pseudonym for Lexi? Or perhaps he really is seeing a woman named Violet. Penelope's thoughts were racing and her body shook with a mixture of adrenaline and fear.

She should have felt like crying right now, but suddenly she felt like doing no such thing. Reaching for her Blackberry, she decided to call her mother. Her friends and family were still in Mellville, and right now she needed someone to talk to.

Penelope's mother, Jeanie, picked up on the third ring. Without giving her a chance to say hello, Penelope opened her mouth and let the whole story spill out. At the very least, her mother's voice could help her abstain from crying right now. But Jeanie did better than that. She told Penelope exactly what she should do.

Chapter Thirteen

When Lexi opened her eyes, she was lying in a hospital bed. It only took a second for her to remember the beating, and she quickly tried to sit up, only to find herself tangled up in a web of IVs and other strange cords.

"Will somebody get me out of these cords!" she yelled as loudly as her sore throat would allow. A nurse came quickly to her aid and pushed her back against the bed with a little more force than necessary.

"Hey, bitch! What do you think you're doing?" Lexi demanded. But the nurse just ignored her. She started checking her IV and messing with other gadgets around the bed.

"Hello!" Lexi tried to say, but it sounded more like a frog croaking. She finally gave up on getting a response from Nurse Ratched, and let her finish whatever job she was supposed to be doing.

"I know you're upset, Mrs. Ambrose, but I assure you the doctors and I are taking good care of you now," Nurse Ratched informed her.

"It's Ms. Ambrose. I'm divorced."

"Okay, Ms. Ambrose."

Nurse Ratched finished fooling around with the IV and took a seat on the edge of the bed. She gave Lexi a stern look that reminded Lexi of her own mother, that is, when her mother was sober.

"Your boyfriend beat you pretty badly. I don't know how much you remember, but you were very lucky."

"You call this lucky?" Lexi croaked. "I feel like dog shit, lady."

"I can imagine that you do, Ms. Ambrose. You have a concussion and several of your ribs are broken. Your nose is broken, and, no offense, but not only do you feel like shit, but you look it too."

Nurse Ratched handed her some ice chips to soothe her parched throat and then provided her with a handheld mirror, per Lexi's request.

Lexi groaned. She looked like the bride of Frankenstein, only worse. Both of her eyes were black, and although her nose was covered with gauze, she could tell it was swollen three times its normal size. "I guess my career as a model is over," Lexi whined sarcastically.

Nurse Ratched raised her eyebrows questioningly. Lexi rolled her eyes and attempted to laugh, but every inch of her body hurt too badly. "I'm only kidding," she said. Nurse Ratched leaned in closer and there it was again: the motherly look.

"Well, you're certainly pretty enough to be a model, young lady. And it doesn't take a social worker to figure out that someone like you can do much better than a jerk like that."

"I suppose by *jerk*, you must be referring to Reggie."

"Is that your boyfriend's name?"

"No."

Nurse Ratched raised her eyebrows and gave Lexi a confused look.

Lexi explained, "I don't have a boyfriend. Reggie and I just dated from time to time, and I assure you, he won't be dating anyone anytime soon after I get my hands on his woman-beating ass!"

Nurse Ratched's eyes widened, and then she let out a low, hearty laugh. Her laughter was contagious apparently, because the next thing Lexi knew, she was laughing right along with her.

"Ow! My ribs hurt…"

"And they are going to hurt for quite some time. Broken ribs take time to heal, and you're going to have to take it easy until they do."

Lexi groaned and covered her face with her hands. "I swear I'm going to kill him."

Nurse Ratched shook her head. "You do not have to kill anyone. Your neighbor beat you to the punch. In fact, I probably should not be telling you this, but Reggie is down the hall in intensive care. Apparently, your neighbor downstairs was trying to ignore your screams and mind his own business. But when he heard you stop screaming all of a sudden, he worried you might be dead. Not only did he call the police, but he busted into your apartment and beat the living daylights out of Reggie. There's a chance he might not make it, and if he does, he has a sheriff waiting to arrest him. Either way you look at it, Honey, that boy's fate is sealed."

Lexi smiled at the nurse, whose real name was Betty, according to her tag. "Thanks, Betty," Lexi whispered hoarsely, and she allowed herself to drift back to sleep.

Chapter Fourteen

Michael showed up at eight on the dot. It was a good thing he'd brought two sacks of wine, because Violet had finished off the entire bottle nearly an hour earlier. She was not normally a big drinker, but she had so enjoyed primping for her night with Michael that she had drunk more than she realized while she was getting ready.

Alex would have been irritated by her drunkenness, but Michael found it endearing, and he scooped her up in a big bear hug as soon as he laid eyes on her. Her dress was spectacular, but she'd kicked off the heels an hour ago because they were killing her feet. But that didn't stop her from putting them on for Michael, and she spun around in a drunken circle, singing "Ta da!"

She did not get to show off the dress for long because the next thing she knew, he was taking it off of her. She had decided on a bra and panty set instead of a negligee, and as he pulled her back, he examined the lacy bra and low-cut thong.

"Wow! Violet, you are gorgeous," he moaned,

keeping his eyes on her as she spun around again, repeating her performance. Michael was mesmerized by her beauty, and he couldn't help but love her childlike excitement and joy. He reached for her, but she pulled back, and he recognized the seriousness of her expression. "Michael, we have to stop…"

Michael put up a hand to keep her from saying the words he was not yet ready to hear, but she took his hand in hers and pulled him over to the edge of the bed where they could talk.

"I know I'm a little tipsy tonight, but I need to say this first, and I hope it comes out right," Violet said. Michael did not like the sound of it, and he told her so.

She explained, "Michael, I love you. I have loved you since I was a girl. But right now I need to say that if we're going to leave our significant others, it should be for more reasons than our feelings for each other."

"I understand what you are saying, and I feel the same way. I don't want you to leave Alex for me. If you are going to leave him, I want you to do it because you want to. I don't want to break up your marriage and carry that burden with me for the rest of my life," he said.

"Exactly," she said. "You proposed to Penelope for a reason, and I know that your feelings for me are real and true, but you have to figure this out on your own. After today, I don't want to sneak around anymore."

"Me neither…but how am I supposed to just walk away from you after everything that's been said and done between us?" he asked, shaking his head from side to side.

"Alex gets home tomorrow, and in another month, he'll be going back to San Diego to work on another site for two months."

"How do you feel about him coming home?" Michael asked.

Violet sighed, and she could feel the tears coming, so she held up a finger and tucked her knees up to her chest. The anxiety was back with a vengeance, and this was not the time or place for her to fall apart. Despite the reality of the situation, she wanted to enjoy this night with Michael. She wanted to enjoy it as though it were their last night together, because in reality, it very well could be.

She took a deep breath to soothe her nerves, and he held her face gently in his hands. He kissed her neck and shoulders lightly, then moved behind her and started massaging the tension out of her shoulders. God, she loved him. And she wanted to savor this moment forever, regardless of how it would end.

Violet closed her eyes and imagined that day when she was eleven. Michael picking her up off the ground and treating her wounds...Michael sitting on the rooftop of his family home, blasting heavy metal as he took drags off one of his parents' cigarettes...Michael walking up to her outside the bar and telling her everything she had ever wanted to hear from him all these years...and last but not least, this very moment, and all of the other recent encounters they'd had. Violet could not imagine never seeing him again. She could not imagine going back to life as usual with Alex and pretending that nothing had ever happened. But she had to know they were doing the right thing, and they owed it to their spouses not to carry on with their relationship until they were sure of what they wanted.

"You asked me how I feel about Alex coming home..." she finally said.

"Yes?" he asked, continuing to massage every ounce of anxiety out of her body.

"Well, the truth is, I don't know how I feel about it. And that is exactly why I think we should both go home tomorrow and spend the next month figuring out ourselves," she said.

"What does that mean, exactly?" he asked, leaning forward to kiss her right earlobe.

"So, this is my proposal to you," she said, turning around to face him on the bed. "In one month, when Alex leaves for San Diego, I will reserve this same room for us," she said.

"Sounds pretty good so far," he said with a chuckle. She gave him a playful shove and reminded him that she was being serious.

"If you decide you want to continue our relationship, then I want you to show up on that day, one month from now..." she murmured softly.

Violet looked up into Michael's amazing, green eyes to see his reaction. "If that's what you think is best, then I'm on board. Waiting to see you for an entire month will be hell, but you know what they say about fondness making the heart grow stronger," he teased, reaching forward to tickle her.

Violet let him tickle her, and they wrestled for

several minutes on the bed, laughing and teasing one another. She finally won the match and straddled him when she had him pinned on his back. She looked into his eyes once more and said, "I want you to take this seriously, Michael. I care about you and your son very much, and I think you owe it to him and to yourself to think this through before we proceed any further."

Michael pulled her face onto his chest, and they held each other wordlessly for a moment. "I will, Violet. I really will," Michael agreed, softly, "and I want you to do the same with Alex. I don't know the guy, but there must be something special about him if he bagged a hot babe like you," he joked, and then they started wrestling again.

Chapter Fifteen

Four hours and three cheeseburgers later, Penelope was ready to take action. Her mother had suggested that she wait a while before going inside the Filmont Inn, just in case Michael was in there alone waiting on some woman to show up. The last thing she wanted was to bust down the door and find him sitting there watching ESPN with his feet up.

But after four hours of nail-biting torture, she could wait no longer. She had called Angela on her cell phone to let the kids know she was okay, and she prompted them to go to bed. She explained her failure to come home by launching into a ridiculous story about an emergency at work that made no sense at all, even to her, but Angie did not seem concerned. Angela reassured Penelope that they had eaten, taken showers, and brushed their teeth. Penelope could hear Elijah laughing in the background, and she couldn't help but feel a sense of dread as she wondered what would happen next and how it would affect not only her and Michael, but also their children.

Penelope glanced at her reflection in the driver-side mirror and noticed the way the dim lights outside the hotel reflected the thin strips of gray in her hair. *After tonight, I will probably go completely gray*, she thought, leaning her back against the seat and squeezing her eyes shut. She wondered why the hell she was worried about how she looked at a time like this. If Michael was in there with some other woman, she did not give a damn what he thought of her anymore. But she knew that wasn't true; the Jeanie in her was struggling to take over in order to preserve her fragile ego, but she knew how bad it would really hurt to lose Michael. She had wanted this to work so badly. She still wanted it to work. Having a family with security and normalcy was all she had ever wanted, and after Brian died…well, she did not want to think about that right now, either.

But the image of his face floated through her mind anyway, and she remembered what she had forgotten for so long, and that was that she loved Brian deeply. They met in nursing school as classmates, but their relationship rapidly developed into courtship. There were fewer men in their class than women; it was that way in almost every nursing program across the country, so, his immediate interest in Penelope sparked jealousy in many of her female counterparts, and thus, they often alienated her when it came to on-campus gatherings and functions. Penelope was so accustomed to concerning herself with public perception, but she was so in love with Brian that she just didn't care; the less time she spent with her female colleagues was just that much more time she could devote to Brian. She discovered she was pregnant with Angela during the spring semester of their junior year. She considered taking a leave of absence, but her mother was so disappointed by her unplanned pregnancy that leaving school too was just not an option for Penelope. She and Brian got part-time jobs and rented a small cottage not far from campus; they completed their studies, and they raised their daughter all on their own, struggling through it together.

Brian brought out the best in her and she the best in him. Angela was merely a small girl of age eight when he fell over dead in the kitchen. The shock was more than either of them could bear, and instead of working through it with a counselor or seeking some type of aid, Penelope acted like her mother; she dove deeper into her work and had one short-lived romance after another. That was until she met Michael Sinclair, and all of the turmoil inside of her started to rest. Tonight, she felt it toiling inside her again, and she was ready to confront this bastard for causing her to feel this much anger and pain again.

Penelope opened the door and stepped out into the chilly night air. She grabbed her coat and bag from the seat and slipped it on slowly as she did a quick scan of the parking lot. Other than her quick trip down the road to McDonald's, she had been parked outside the hotel all night. She had seen no more signs of Michael, and his Jeep was still as he left it. Other than several families and one lonely looking gentleman, she had not seen anyone else enter the hotel. What she had really been waiting for was some hussy to pull up and go in alone so she could at least identify her target. Penelope had no doubt in her mind that if Michael was meeting someone, that someone had arrived before him and was most likely his ex-wife and Elijah's estranged mother, Lexi.

Penelope's hands curled into fists as she imagined Michael and that stupid slut hooking up again. She had never had the pleasure of meeting the wench, but she had heard stories aplenty about Lexi Ambrose. Lexi had been pretty wild back in the day, and Penelope knew that Lexi and Michael had experimented with drugs and indulged in promiscuous sex. *The fact that she would abandon her only son speaks volumes about her character, not only as a mother but also as a person*, Penelope thought with a smirk.

Even though she did not know Michael before two years ago, she had done her homework on him as well. His reputation for wildness had scared her at first, but she had to admit that it was also what appealed to her most. He was mysterious and dark at times, and she loved going out with him and watching women drool over him. Not only that, but he was also a single father with an established career, and he was great with Elijah. He was great with Angela too, she reminded herself. Her heart ached at the thought of seeing Angie lose another father figure in her life.

Penelope sighed and took a deep breath before opening the door to the lobby of the Filmont Inn.

She had never been here before, and she had to admit it was quite lovely. She headed for the check-in counter, trying to look confident and innocent of any wrongdoing. The receptionist greeted her with a smile and asked if she needed a room for the night. "No, thank you. I'm here to meet my fiancé, Michael Sinclair. He checked in around eight this evening, and I was supposed to meet him after work, but I was running late," Penelope quickly improvised.

"Room number?" the receptionist asked, looking up at Penelope with a smile.

"Ugh…shit, I don't remember. I think it was on the second floor, maybe. Damn…"

Penelope pulled out her Blackberry and pretended to dial Michael's number. She held the phone to her ear and said, "I was hoping not to wake him, but I guess I'll have to call up and see…"

A family of four walked up behind her, and Penelope cursed loudly as she hung up the phone and fake-dialed him again. The mother behind her gave her a disapproving glance and the next thing she knew, she was being handed a room key. "Enjoy your stay, ma'am," the annoying receptionist told her, eager to get her out of there before she scared off any new customers.

Penelope gave a sigh of relief, as she pressed the button for the elevator. As she waited, she noticed the silver trash can that sat in the center of both doorways. She stole a glance down at the keycard in her hand.

"Room 206, here I come," she boasted aloud, and then she pulled the model airplane and the box of Lexi and Michael memorabilia from her bag, tossing them in the trash just as the elevator doors opened wide for her grand entrance.

Chapter Sixteen

Even though it was past midnight and she was curled up with the sexiest man on the planet, Violet could not sleep. She was overwhelmed with thoughts of Michael, his family, and her own husband who was due home in approximately fourteen hours. It was hard to believe that by this time tomorrow night, she would probably be lying in bed next to Alex instead of Michael. She stroked Michael's hair and stole a glance at his peaceful, sleeping face. He was snoring softly, and she wished she could do the same.

Violet finally gave in to the restlessness and pulled herself out of bed, being careful not to wake up Michael. She went into the hotel bathroom. She brushed her teeth and washed her face. She smiled as she thought about how perfect the evening had been. Michael and she had made love for hours and then finished off the champagne and chocolates. After that, he carried her to the large Jacuzzi tub where he washed her hair and scrubbed her back. Looking back, the night felt like a dream. When it came to her attraction to Michael, it wasn't just about the sex. Of course the sex was great, but in addition to being a tremendous lover, he was also a wonderful friend. Over the past few months, they had shared more deep conversations than she had shared with everyone she had ever known combined. He was charming, funny, and loyal.

Loyal seemed like a strange way to describe him, considering his infidelity. Perhaps she was being naïve, but she knew it wasn't in Michael's nature to hurt people, and despite his feelings for her, she could tell he was tormented by his current situation.

While taking a bath, Michael had opened up with her about his current relationship. Violet refrained from saying anything negative about Penelope. After all, she had never met the woman, and one of her greatest pet peeves was catty women who liked nothing better than to bash one another.

Michael had a lot of good things to say about Penelope. She was pretty much the exact opposite of his first wife. She was responsible, grounded, and matronly. She liked him home for dinner by seven, and she attended all of her daughter's cheerleading games diligently.

Violet could tell he had reached a sore spot in the story when he started to talk about Penelope's daughter, Angela. Angela had been fatherless since the age of six, and apparently, she and Michael's son, Elijah, had really hit it off. Although he described his relationship with Angela as rocky at first, it became apparent that both Angela and Michael had grown attached to each other over the past year. And then there was Elijah…

Michael broke down when he talked about the years that it had just been he and Elijah. It was obvious he felt horrible for every mistake he had made along the way. Michael admitted that he had felt awkward comforting his son after Lexi left. He could barely take care of himself, much less a small child, he admitted. Violet could see the shame in his eyes as he talked on and on about missed birthdays, bouncing Elijah around from one babysitter to the next, and teaching the boy to basically fend for himself on nights when he was working late.

Michael's humility was one thing she loved about him. Despite his confident demeanor and dashing good looks, he was just as damaged and insecure as she, if not more so.

Violet tried to reassure Michael that he had raised Elijah the best way he knew how and that she admired his courage after experiencing the devastating loss of his wife and his son's mother. She told him something she once heard her Granny say: "Bad parents don't sit around wondering if they are bad parents. So, anytime I hear a parent questioning their skills or ruminating over something they should have done, or could have done better for their children, I know right away that they're good parents. Bad parents do not know that they're bad parents because they don't care enough about their children to stop and question themselves."

Michael had fallen asleep watching an old western shortly after eleven. She loved watching him sleep, and she wondered if he was dreaming. She prayed that if he was, the dreams were good ones.

Violet used the bathroom and headed over to the small dinette table that was located next to the TV set. She felt inspired to write down some ideas for her book and regretted not bringing her laptop.

She flipped on the small reading light next to the table and found a pad of paper and pens in one of the desk drawers. She settled down into a chair and lit a cigarette before jotting down a few notes she could refer to later when she got home to her computer.

Violet's thoughts were quickly disturbed by a sound at the door. It almost sounded like someone was turning the knob. Perhaps some intoxicated person had come to their door by mistake. *After all, this is a hotel*, she thought.

She tried to focus her thoughts back to her writing, but then she heard what sounded like a keycard sliding in the lock, and the next thing she knew, some blonde woman threw open the hotel room door and charged right at her.

Chapter Seventeen

The first thing Penelope saw when she opened the door to Room 206 was a half-naked broad sitting at a table and her completely naked fiancé in bed. This woman sitting in the chair was not Lexi Ambrose. Without a second thought, she ran straight at her, knocking her out of the chair and waking up Michael in the process. Penelope's first instinct was to hurt this woman, but on second thought, she would much rather hurt the person who was really responsible for inflicting all of this pain: Michael Sinclair.

Michael was sitting up in the bed now, and she hurtled herself toward him, slapping at his face frantically. "How could you do this to me, Michael?" she screamed, "to my daughter...your son..." she exclaimed breathily. "I feel so...broken," she finished.

Michael was out of bed now, and he was holding her around the waist. She no longer had the energy to fight anyone. She felt hopelessly defeated, and all she wanted to do was lie down and give up.

The door to the room was open, and by now, people were coming out of their rooms in response to the commotion. Most of the hotel patrons were perfectly content to just stand near the doorway watching this drama unfold. *They are vultures*, Penelope thought, and she felt utter disgust for them and for her own behavior. Her mother had told her to go in there and just keep her head high as she confronted Michael, and this was definitely not what she had in mind. She was making a spectacle of herself.

"Penelope, p-please...let me get dressed, and I'll drive you home," Michael stammered. The whole scenario seemed so unreal to him, like a terrible nightmare he had suddenly woken up from—only this was his reality, and he had to deal with it.

Michael told Penelope to wait in the hallway so he could get dressed, and she surprisingly complied, sliding down the wall outside the doorframe and crying with her head hung low to her knees. The look on her face was pure devastation, and Michael was responsible for it.

***

Michael closed the hotel room door and turned around to find Violet, fully dressed, with her suitcase in one hand and her purse in the other. "Violet, I'm so sorry. I don't know how she found out..." he apologized.

"I'm sorry too, Michael," she responded softly, and she kissed his mouth before walking past him and out the front door. Michael couldn't help but wonder if it was the last time he would ever see her again. He buried his face in his hands and began sobbing so loudly that even Penelope sat up in surprise from her place on the floor in the hallway.

Penelope watched her husband's mistress walk away from Room 206, and she wondered if this would be their last encounter. Her anger had subsided, and now all she could feel was a deep, painful sadness. Instead of waiting for Michael as he had instructed, she followed Violet's lead and left Michael alone in his hotel room.

Chapter Eighteen

In the movies, sneaking out of a hospital always seems like such an insurmountable task that involves dressing up in nurses' uniforms and tiptoeing past security guards. But Lexi just removed the IV, threw on the bloodstained clothes she had arrived in, and walked out the front door of the hospital. "Piece of cake," she said with a painful smile. The hardest part about her *escape* was not the challenge of making it out unnoticed, but making it out at all, considering how much pain she was in. Her ribs ached like crazy, and she felt like she was carrying a ninety-pound barbell on her neck. Every inch of her hurt, but there was no way she was staying in the hospital, not with Reggie right down the hall from her. Nurse Betty had reported he was in intensive care, but you never know about some people, and she didn't want him waking up and trying to kill her again—not to mention the fact that strip clubs don't offer insurance, and she did not want to endure any unpleasant discussions about the mounting medical bills she had undoubtedly racked up during her hospital stay.

Lying alone in that hospital bed, she had made the decision to get the hell out of this town. She wanted to get in her car and just drive away, leaving everything and everyone she'd met here behind. Nothing and nobody here mattered. There were only two people that mattered to her: Michael and Elijah Sinclair. And although they seemed to be worlds apart, in reality, they were only a three-hour plane ride away. *What have I got to lose at this point?* Lexi wondered.

Lexi had not been a part of Elijah's life in nearly ten years, and she would not blame him if he never wanted to see or hear from her again. *I hope the airplane I sent didn't hurt him worse*, she thought, thinking of how she'd impulsively mailed it out days ago.

I hope it wasn't a mistake.

Lexi was so deep in thought that it took her a minute to realize everyone around her was staring. She was standing outside the hospital emergency room entrance. She remembered the blood on her clothes, and oh God…how could she forget about her busted up face? She grabbed a pair of sunglasses from her satchel. Not only did they help conceal her face, but they also kept the sun from glaring into her eyes. That was a blessing considering the fact that she could barely hold her eyes open at all due to the massive swelling.

Lexi was grateful to see a sandwich shop and small department store across the street from the hospital. She was so hungry her stomach felt like it was eating itself, but she opted for the department store first. She grabbed the first t-shirt that she saw and grabbed a pair of jeans off a table by the cash register. The cashier was not fooled by the sunglasses and looked mildly alarmed by Lexi's appearance. For a moment, Lexi worried she might call the cops. But she just rang up the items, took her money, and placed her items in a small paper bag.

"Have a great day!" Lexi half-shouted sarcastically, picking up her bag from the counter. The girl looked scared to death, and Lexi gave her a small wave as she headed out. Lexi changed into her new clothes in the sandwich shop bathroom; then she ordered the biggest, greasiest burger on the menu. The meal came with fries and a soft drink, and she had all but finished off the fries and Coke by the time her sandwich was done. *I guess my eyes were larger than my belly*, she thought. She asked for a doggie bag and tucked the burger inside it.

The pain in her face and ribs was getting more and more intense, and she felt as though she might pass out when she stepped out of the sandwich shop and back into the sunlight. She wandered two more blocks until she saw the park, and she perched on a concrete bench and lit up a cigarette. The nicotine felt good, and now all she needed was a big dose of Tylenol and a nap.

Lexi dozed for nearly an hour on the concrete bench. Unsurprisingly, she felt even worse when she awoke, and she regretted sleeping on such an awkward, hard surface. She gathered up her satchel and doggie bag and headed out in search of a pharmacy. Tylenol was a must-have. Her head was pounding. There was a time in her life when she would have craved something stronger not only to ease her physical discomfort but also to numb the deep-seated emotional pain that she felt on a daily basis. But those days were long gone thanks to an extended stint in rehab and her ever-growing desire to punish herself for leaving the only man she would ever love and her darling son. Lexi hated herself. No amount of drugs or mind-numbing activities could ever change that.

Lexi would never forget the day she left them. It was a dreary day, cloud-filled and stormy as she paid the babysitter to keep Elijah until Michael returned home. She had crammed as many clothes as possible into a grimy, old duffel bag she kept in her closet. That day, when she left, she did not leave a note for her husband, and she did not kiss her small son goodbye. The intense withdrawals had overtaken her body and mind, and her yearning for heroin outweighed her love that day. Michael had given her an ultimatum; now that they had children, she had to either give up the drugs voluntarily, or he was determined to take her to some sort of rehab facility. Her craving for the drug and relentless ignorance of how bad her addiction had truly become had driven her away from them. She went off on her own with her own truth at the time, which was a needle and a small brown bag tucked beneath her trousers.

Years went by, and she lived that way: the life of a junkie, the life of a whore. Looking back, she did not know that person: that strung out girl who did not weigh ninety pounds soaking wet and who loved getting high more than she loved her own family. That girl was a stranger to her now. She was saved by an elderly gentleman, a former addict himself, who took her into his very own home and fed her Suboxone strips until she no longer felt the aches and chills of withdrawal. That man died shortly after her recovery, and she wept at his funeral. He was the closest thing to a real father Lexi had ever known.

As Lexi started to cross the street, she froze at the sight of Gabriel Calcutta, one of Reggie's cronies. Actually, he was more like a dealer than a friend. Lexi turned around and ducked behind the nearest building. She waited for several minutes before working up the nerve to venture back around the building. Gabriel appeared to be gone, and she highly doubted he could have recognized her with the baggy new clothes and enormous nose. She tried to laugh, but it only hurt worse.

Fuck the Tylenol. She had to get the hell out of this city. It would only be a matter of time before one of Reggie's buddies found out about what had happened, and she did not put it past them to finish her off for good on Reggie's behalf.

Lexi didn't care where she went as long as it was far away from here. As eager as she was to get away, she couldn't leave just yet. She needed to gather a few of her meager belongings from the apartment and fish out a small roll of emergency money that she had sealed in a sandwich baggy hidden in the tank of her toilet. There was another piece of unfinished business to resolve, and she wasn't looking forward to it one little bit.

Chapter Nineteen

Violet woke up in her car. The morning sunshine was burning her face, and her back was slick with sweat from lying on the tan leather seat of her Geo Tracker. She groaned as she thought about Michael and what had transpired the day before. *Did that really happen?* she wondered.

One look at her face held the answer to that question. Her cheeks were stained with dark makeup and she had ugly, dark circles under her eyes from being awake all night. "Damn," she said out loud as she imagined Penelope charging straight for her like a bull to a red flag.

Violet reached for the Tylenol she kept in the glove box and washed down three tablets with an old can of Mountain Dew. *Well, at least I finally got to meet Penelope*, she thought with a tired grin. She suddenly realized what day it was. Alex was coming home. She turned the car on and was shocked to see that the dashboard clock read 10:00 AM. She rarely slept past seven, but after the night she'd had who could blame her for feeling a tad more fatigued than usual? She had pulled away from the Filmont Inn in so much distress and under the influence of the champagne that she had pulled over in a nearby parking lot. She had tossed and turned, and cried, until she felt too dehydrated to cry anymore.

Alex would be home in the next four hours as long as his flight arrived on time. She put the car into gear and pulled out of the lot. It was finally time to head home. She needed a bath. She wasn't ready to face Alex tonight. In fact, she wasn't sure if she was even ready to face the day in general.

Violet squealed to a halt as she emerged over the hill leading up to her house. Her mouth fell open, and she shook her head in disbelief. *Could things get any worse?* she wondered.

There it was—Alex's truck in the driveway. Apparently he was home early. *This is just great,* she thought miserably as she put the car in park and turned off the ignition. She reached in the backseat for her suitcase, but then she remembered the new dress and lingerie and decided it was best to just leave it in the car for now.

Violet's mind was spinning as she slowly ascended up the front walk and turned the knob to the grand old home. After several months, she was going to see Alex again. Boy, did he sure pick a bad time to come home.

Chapter Twenty

Lexi had never been so happy to see the Malibu before. She patted its hood with a triumphant smile. She'd thought for sure it would have been towed away by now considering the illegal spot where she had left it. But there it was looking as rusty and old as ever.

Lexi borrowed a telephone book from a clerk at the gas station down the street and used a payphone to call for a tow truck.

The tow truck arrived fairly quickly, and Lexi gave him all of the cash she had on hand to haul the Malibu to the nearest auto shop to replace her tire. "Make sure to tell Antonio that I will pick it up in a few weeks when I get back to town. He knows I'm good for it," she said.

"Sure thing, honey," the driver assured her.

On any other day, Lexi would have responded to his *honey* with a snarky comment. But this was a new day. She was a new woman now with a brand new attitude to boot.

Since she was out of cash, it was time to go to

her apartment. She was not looking forward to it, and the last thing she needed was a run-in with one of Reggie's goons. However, her emergency cash stash was there along with all of her clothes, toiletries, and mementos. There was no way she was leaving her stuff behind.

But before she caught the bus to her apartment, she had another stop to make. The Clamshell's sign was off since it was daytime, but they weren't closed. The Clamshell never closed. *Kind of like hell*, Lexi thought drearily.

Lexi nodded to Charlie as she strolled through the door. He looked surprised to see her and even more surprised by her battered face. She flashed him the most sincere smile she could muster.

She headed straight to the back to retrieve her makeup, costumes, and toiletries. Lexi had assumed all of her things would be cleared from her station by now and either thrown away or divided up among the other dancers, but she was pleased to see that everything was just as she had left them.

Lexi grabbed one of her costume bags off its hook beside her mirror and started tossing all of her stuff inside. She wanted to get in and out as quickly as possible before Billy showed up and bawled her out for her recent absences from work.

Three of her fellow dancers were sitting at their stations, and not a one of them said hello, or even glanced her way. She felt pissed off, which was silly considering the fact that no one here was her friend, and she'd probably never see any of these girls ever again. It's not that Lexi disliked them, and in fact, she had hoped to find a friend or two when she started dancing at the Clamshell. Unfortunately, like most other women she knew, these girls viewed each other as adversaries instead of comrades. *We always turn on each other because we view one another as competition*, Lexi thought sadly. *But what the hell are we competing for, anyway?* she wondered. The last time she checked, men were the only ones who seemed to have a leg up in life in comparison to women. *So, why don't we join forces, and instead of looking for our differences, why don't we appreciate all of the commonalities we share?*

Lexi stopped philosophizing and finished packing the last bit of her stuff into her costume bag. She started to head for the door but then had a thought and turned back to her now-empty work station. She pulled a tube of red lipstick out of her bag and used it to write on the vanity mirror above her station. First she wrote:

Billy—I quit!

After that she wrote nine more messages, one for each of her soon-to-be former dance mates. She wrote something nice about every single one of them and finished off with a sloppy,

It was a pleasure working with every single one of you. I wish you all the best of luck, and I'm sorry for not trying harder to be a friend to all of you. Dance on, ladies!

With that said, she draped her costume bag over her shoulder and walked out of the Clamshell for the last time. Billy was standing at the bar, and he called out after her, but she just gave him the finger and kept on walking. She started humming the lyrics of that old, catchy, pop song recorded by Nancy Sinatra.

"These boots are made for walking...and that's just what they'll do..."

Pretty soon these boots will be boarding a plane making their way back home to my boys! Lexi thought happily.

Chapter Twenty-One

After leaving the Filmont Inn, Penelope had driven around for an hour before finally deciding there was nowhere to go but home. When she got home, she looked in on the kids and lay awake in bed all night without sleeping. She had hoped Michael would come home after both she and his mistress had left him at the hotel, but he had never shown up.

Penelope's eyes were still open when her alarm went off at six o'clock. The alarm continued to beep as she stared blankly at the crown molding that bordered her bedroom ceiling. The bedroom was a sandy brown, and she remembered it was one of the reasons she had picked this house. It seemed so silly now, picking a house because of a paint color…to think that only a few short months ago her greatest concerns were picking paint colors and draperies.

Penelope remembered how content Michael seemed, and despite his complaints about the cookie cutter designs of the neighborhood, she could tell he was excited to live in such a beautiful, spacious home. She imagined Angie's face that day as she jumped out of the car to look at every home with a For Sale sign in the yard, and no matter how big or small the home, each one was "The One," according to Angie.

Penelope thought about her first date with Michael and how she had dreaded meeting him because the date was arranged by mutual friends of theirs, and everybody knows how most blind dates turn out. Penelope and Michael had an immediate connection. Images of his proposal danced through her mind, taunting her.

She remembered how happy she felt when he got down on one knee and asked her to marry him in front of their family and friends at Thanksgiving. She had been taken by complete surprise, and in fact, it had taken several seconds for her to finally remember she was supposed to give him an answer. She shouted out, "Yes!" and burst into tears of utter joy as he slipped the beautiful diamond ring on her finger. Just like a scene from a romance novel, she remembered sadly.

"Mom, your alarm is going off! It's driving us crazy!" Angie shouted through the door.

Penelope jumped up with a start at the sound of her daughter's voice, and she reached over to turn off the alarm. "Get ready for school, guys!" she hollered as she swung her legs over the side of the bed and stood up to put on her robe. *That's the thing about being a mom*, Penelope thought. No matter what is going on in your life, you still get up and play your role of mom. *That's one lesson I can thank my own mother for*. She actually smiled slightly before remembering that her role of wife was about to change significantly. She headed for the bathroom to brush her teeth. Like usual, she removed her engagement ring before wetting her brush out of fear that it would slide from her finger and escape down the sink drain. Without thinking twice about it, she picked up the ring and did exactly that. She watched it swirl around the sink until it edged its way to the drain in the middle of the basin.

Chapter Twenty-Two

Seeing Alex's truck in the driveway felt like a punch in the gut. He was sitting on the sofa in the great room when she came through the door. The daily newspaper was on his lap, but he did not appear to be reading. He was looking straight ahead at the flames that danced in the fireplace. "Alex?" she called out, wondering if he was asleep or deep in thought. He's definitely awake, she realized as he turned around with an ugly expression on his face.

"Where have you been all night, Violet?" he boomed, his voice echoing off the high cathedral ceilings.

Violet was shocked by his anger and the sheer volume of his voice, and she stammered, "A-Alex, I—" but he quickly cut her off.

"I got here yesterday around three o'clock in the afternoon. I wanted to surprise you, and that's why I insisted you not pick me up from the airport. Do you even realize why I planned to come home yesterday instead of today? Well, do you?" he hollered again.

Who was this person? she wondered. She had half a mind to just turn and run back out the front door.

"Alex, I have no idea why you decided to come home early. You could have at least told me…" she said in a quiet voice that sounded almost like a whisper. "I was at work, Alex…" she tried to continue, but he held up his hand.

"Stop."

His voice was lower now and his expression softened. "You were not at work yesterday. I checked the library, and I called your coworkers." His gaze drifted back to the fire.

"Alex, I'm sorry," she murmured, taking a few steps toward the couch. "I don't know what to say right now except that I'm sorry…"

Alex sighed, and when their eyes met, she saw that his eyes were red from crying. "Yesterday was April sixth. I pushed the flight up a day so I could come home to be with you for our one-year wedding anniversary…" he said.

Violet shook her head in disbelief. How could she have forgotten the date? Instead of celebrating her anniversary with her husband, she had been lying in a hotel room with an engaged man—not to mention the way the night had ended with his scorned fiancée charging into the room.

She felt ashamed for hurting Alex like this. Regardless of how unhappy she felt with the relationship, he was still a person that deserved to be treated with respect. He did not deserve to be cheated on or lied to regardless of what he'd done or hadn't done while working out of state.

"You deserve better, Alex," she heard herself say. Then she turned and headed back out the way she had come in—only this time she left behind her wedding ring on the table.

Chapter Twenty-Three

Angela extended her arms into a V and smiled brightly out at the crowd. *The routine was a hit,* she thought, beaming up at her mother as the crowd roared with whistles and applause.

Angela loved the way sound traveled in a gymnasium, with the cheers reverberating again and again as though she were standing in the middle of a canyon. It was game night at Riverside High and Angela's debut as the newest member of the junior varsity cheerleading squad. Overall, she would deem the night a success. Her soon-to-be stepbrother, Elijah, was leading the boys' basketball team in points; they were up by twelve, and it was only halftime.

Now that the halftime show was over, people were making their way down the bleachers for bathroom breaks and snacks. Angela headed up the bleachers to see her mother, Penelope.

***

As Penelope watched Angie approach, she could not help but feel content with how her life had turned out. Nearly two days had passed since the incident at the Filmont Inn with Michael, and she had not seen or heard from him at all. Despite all of that, she felt overjoyed watching her beautiful daughter on her first night as a Riverside cheerleader. Angela was the best thing that had ever happened to her. Even after losing her first husband, Brian, to a heart attack and then catching her new fiancé cheating, Penelope realized that she was lucky to have such a lovely, kind-hearted, and intelligent daughter.

For a moment, Penelope imagined what life would be like if it were just her and Angie: no man, no big house, just the two of them. *We would be just fine*, Penelope realized, and she draped her arm around her daughter's shoulder as Angie took a seat beside her on the bleachers. "I'm so proud of you, Honey," Penelope told her, fighting the urge to become tearful.

***

Angela felt relieved to see her mother smile because even though her mother thought she was naïve, she could tell something had been bothering her all week. Elijah could sense it too. According to Penelope, Elijah's father, Michael, had been working all night the past two nights, and that was why he had not been home. Elijah and Angie were skeptical. Even though Angie didn't like to think her mother was lying to her, she admired and appreciated her mother's ability to stay strong and never worry her or Elijah with "grown-up" problems.

Just then the buzzer sounded, and the basketball team emerged from the locker room. Once again, the gymnasium was filled with cheers and whoops of excitement. Elijah was in the front of the pack, and he smiled and waved up at them. Angela had to admit he was adorable, and a part of her wished their parents were not planning to marry, because in another life maybe they could have been an item. She instantly felt silly for thinking such thoughts. "Gotta get back out there, Mom!"

***

Penelope patted her daughter on the back and then watched her descend the bleachers and join her squad on the sidelines. Her eyes drifted over to the floor to where Elijah stood stretching his arm and calf muscles. He was the spitting image of his father, and even though he was not her biological son, she did adore him, and she would have been lucky to have him as her own. Of all the surprises she had endured this week, the one that surprised her the most was Michael's absence from his son's first basketball game of the season. *He deserves to have someone cheering for him*, she thought angrily, *but on second thought, he does. He has me.* She clapped her hands together and yelled, "Come on, Elijah! Let's go!"

The Riverside Pirates were victorious, and when the game was over, Penelope congratulated Elijah and Angela on a job well done. She was proud of them both. Penelope suggested they go out for pizza to celebrate, but they were quick to remind her that they already had plans of their own. Elijah had plans to stay over at his best friend Pete's house, and Angie was going to have a sleepover with several of her new teammates.

Penelope hugged them both, and after watching them head off with their friends, she made her way across the school parking lot and climbed into the Escalade. She wondered if and when Michael would return home, and felt depressed as she anticipated going home to an empty house and an even emptier bed.

As Penelope edged the SUV out of its parking space, she almost didn't see the dark-haired woman step out in front of her. Luckily, Penelope reacted quickly and pressed down on the brake. For a moment their eyes met, and Penelope could have sworn that the woman very closely resembled Michael's ex-wife, Lexi.

Wow, I really must be losing it, Penelope thought, shaking her head. *First, I think she's the one having an affair with Michael, and now I think I'm seeing her everywhere*, she thought warily. The woman waved apologetically and kept walking, her head tucked in to her chest.

Chapter Twenty-Four

Lexi was so distracted that she nearly let herself get run over by an SUV. Tonight, after eight long years, she had finally seen her son, Elijah. Even after all these years, he was impossible to miss. He was the spitting image of his father.

The first thing Lexi did when she arrived in town was take a cab to Michael and Elijah's last known place of residence in Oaksdale. It didn't take long to figure out that they no longer lived there after she was greeted at the door by an elderly Asian couple.

Honestly, did I really expect them to still be there? Lexi wondered. So much time had passed, and with time comes change. However, she knew Michael like the back of her hand, and he was nothing if not consistent when it came to raising Elijah. She suspected that Michael still lived somewhere in Oaksdale—not only because it was his childhood home, but because he wanted Elijah to attend school at Riverside. Lexi could remember how set Michael had been on the idea of sending their son to Riverside. It was his alma mater, and he held the school's reputation in high regard.

Lexi had paid the cabbie and set him free, opting to head out on foot. She stopped first at a local mom and pop convenience store to buy a soda and get her thoughts together. It was there she saw his name on the front page of the local newspaper.

It was a headline advertising the Pirates' first basketball game of the season, and the name Elijah Sinclair was second on the list under a fuzzy team picture. "Are these free?" she asked the boy working the counter, and headed out of the store without waiting for his response.

Lexi spent nearly an hour sitting on an old picnic table studying the photograph that contained a snapshot of her only son. The picture was unclear and poorly shot, but her finger quickly rested on the small, round face of Elijah Sinclair. She would recognize that smile anywhere. She was mesmerized by the photo and could have spent all day memorizing the handsome features that made up her son's face, but she had somewhere to go.

There was a cheap motel four blocks from Riverside High School, one of those pay-by-the-day type deals. She paid for a room and accepted her key, then headed back out on foot toward the school. It was opening night of the season, and she had a ball game to watch.

Lexi had never been a fan of sports, but as she watched Elijah Sinclair dribble that ball and put it through the hoop, she fell in love with basketball. More so, she fell in love with watching him and every little movement that he made. To think that she had actually played a part in creating such a strong, handsome boy made her feel an overwhelming sense of pride. She had to give Michael all of the credit for raising him on his own, but she loved knowing that her body had cultivated and held this lovely young man.

Lexi had chosen a seat at the top of the bleachers so she could stay far enough back from the court to not be spotted. She knew that even if she had been spotted, it would not make a difference. Elijah didn't know her anymore, and unfortunately, she barely knew him either. At halftime, her eyes scanned the crowd for Michael, but surprisingly, he wasn't there. *That seems odd*, she thought, wondering why the boy's father would not be here on such an important night. That seemed so unlike the Michael she remembered. Even though she primarily came to see her son, she had been hoping to see Michael as well. There was a time when they were not only lovers but best friends. She had missed him nearly as much as her son, and she had to admit that she yearned to see him.

After the game, she saw Elijah talking to his friends and a few adults, but still no Michael. Elijah seemed happy, and for a moment, Lexi wondered if maybe she should simply return to her hotel, pack her belongings, and leave things just as they were. But seeing Elijah was like a dream—one she never wanted to end. But the game was over, and the last thing Elijah needed right now was a surprise reunion with his long lost mother, so she headed out of the gymnasium and crossed the parking lot with her head down.

Her walk back to the motel was a slow one. It

felt bittersweet. She still felt giddy with excitement from seeing her son, but those old feelings of guilt and sadness were creeping back in. Leaving Michael, and most of all, Elijah, was the stupidest thing she had ever done, and she knew it. She was unsure of how to fix things, or if it was even remotely possible, but unlike the last time, she was not giving up.

Regardless of how long she had been gone, one thing was crystal clear: Lexi was never going to leave again. Even if Michael hated her and Elijah never wanted to see her, she wanted to remain close, if only for moments like tonight when she could briefly capture a small glimpse of Elijah's life…even if it was from afar.

Chapter Twenty-Five

Like a thief in the night, Alex was there one moment and gone the next. After staying with her sister for a few days, Violet returned to find his clothing and personal items gone. The only trace of his recent presence in the house was a small, handwritten note lying on the bed of the newly converted room in the attic. It read:

Dear Violet,

You are, and always will be, the girl of my dreams. All I have ever wanted is to make you proud of me. When I accepted this job out of state, it was my attempt to go out on my own and save money for us to start a real life together. You know that old saying, "Absence makes the heart grow fonder"? Well, unfortunately, in our case, it pulled us apart. I'm sorry that I ever left. I'm not sure if it's that you love someone else, or perhaps you just no longer love me, but either way, I can tell by the look in your eyes that something has changed. I am going on to San Diego to start the job early. This will give you time to sort out your feelings. If you change your mind and want me to return home, I will. Hell, I'll even quit my job if you want me to, Violet. Regardless of your decision, you should keep the house. It has always been your dream house and perhaps, with or without me, your dreams will come true inside of it. I love you. Alex

Violet folded the note into a tiny square, tucked it away in her jeans pocket, and laid down belly-first on the bed. She didn't cry. She wasn't sure why the tears didn't come, but she did feel sadness…sadness for hurting her husband and sadness for the end of a dream: the idea of a marriage that had once seemed like such a splendid venture, filled with happiness and planning.

The truth is, Alex does deserve better, Violet realized. *He deserves to have someone love him as much as I love Michael, and someone who wants to marry him as much as he wants to marry me.*

For Violet, cooking was like therapy, and there never seemed a greater need for it than now. She headed to the kitchen to scope out available ingredients, finally settling on a strawberry cake after she spotted a carton of fresh strawberries in the refrigerator.

In a large bowl she blended the cream, butter, sugar, and dry strawberry gelatin. Then she beat four eggs and stirred until her hands ached. Now all that was left to do was create the purée and prepare for baking.

Violet glanced at the clock. She had just enough time to finish the cake and get dressed before heading in for her shift at the library. Saturdays were usually busy, and that sounded like a good thing for her right now. The best way to clear her mind was to fill it with every day, mindless activities like sorting books and pulling library cards for its patrons.

My colleagues will love me for bringing this in. Violet smiled down at the cake as she popped it in the oven and set a timer. As she showered and dressed, Violet couldn't help but think about how big and empty the house would feel without a husband or children to fill it. *Perhaps buying this old place was a huge mistake,* Violet wondered grumpily. Not only that, but the utility bills were outrageous, and even though she could make it on her own financially, it would not be an easy task. When she made the decision to buy it, she had never planned on taking care of it all by herself.

Maybe I should get a roommate, she considered. She slipped on her shoes and headed back downstairs to check the timer. She couldn't help but imagine what it would be like to live with Michael Sinclair, but moving in together any time in the future was an unrealistic idea. They had not spoken in days, and although waiting a month to decide on their feelings didn't seem like much time, it seemed like an eternity to Violet. Furthermore, Alex's written words resonated through her mind; what if time apart made her and Michael grow apart too?

In the meantime, maybe she could rent out some space to a roommate. It actually sounded kind of fun, but Violet couldn't really think of any family, friends, or colleagues that needed a space. Still considering the idea, she pulled the cake from the oven, slathered on the purée, and dashed out the door for work.

Chapter Twenty-Six

The rattling of keys in the doorway should have been enough to wake her, but on a day like today, Penelope was just too tired to care. Sleep had not come easy last night, and it was nearly dawn by the time her brain finally shut off and permitted her eyes to do the same. With the kids at their friends' houses and Michael who knows where, she should have been able to spend a Saturday morning in bed, maybe sleeping in for once, or at the very least, sulking alone. But today, she had no such luck. There was someone coming in the front door.

Penelope was sprawled out on the living room couch when Jeanie Pinkerton stepped over the threshold.

"I'll be damned..." Penelope's mother swore. She shook her head disapprovingly as her eyes scanned over the untidy living area, finally resting on her daughter's shiftless form on the couch. "This place is a pig sty, Penelope! Just because you have a no-good man in your life, it doesn't mean you have to just...well, give up on yourself." Her voice was traced with disdain.

Penelope groaned and rolled over. "I am not giving up, Mother!" She pulled herself up from the couch. "What are you doing here?" Penelope asked angrily.

"I've been ringing the doorbell for a good ten minutes, so I decided to use my key. You are, in fact, the one who gave me the key. As I recall, you said I was welcome to use it whenever I wanted," her mother replied, picking up clothes and leftover dishes as she talked. Jeanie saw the look on her daughter's face and stopped cleaning. She sighed and took a seat on the couch. "I'm just worried about you, Honey."

Penelope's anger subsided. On a normal day, her house would have been tidy. And on a normal day, she would have been up and dressed and busying herself with whatever tasks she deemed important that day. But today was not a normal day; it was a downright shitty day. Today she was going to have to tell her daughter the truth—that Michael probably wasn't coming back, and that once again a father figure that had entered her life would be leaving it unexpectedly.

It was unusual for Penelope to have a meaningful heart to heart with her mother, and in fact, she couldn't think of any time they had had such talks. But today, she shared her thoughts with her mother.

"What should I do, Mom?" Penelope whined.

"What do you want to do, honey? What do you think would make you most happy?" Jeanie asked her daughter.

"Michael makes me happy," Penelope replied

softly. She sat there for a moment, chewing her lip. "I have to get him back, Mom."

Chapter Twenty-Seven

After spending the day looking for a job, Lexi couldn't help feeling discouraged. Oaksdale was a small town, and the few places that were hiring required more experience than she had to offer. *Who am I kidding?* Lexi wondered. *Who, in this town, is going to hire an ex-stripper with a bruised-up face? Ugh, I am utterly pathetic and no one is going to hire me.* Lexi wanted to be a part of Elijah and Michael's lives, if he would have her, but she was not foolish enough to approach them without a job or a place to live.

Lexi's feet ached as she walked to her pay-by-the-day motel room. Even though she was used to being on her feet all day, she wasn't used to walking miles up and down the city of Oaksdale, especially with a set of broken ribs. She was unknown to most of its city's residents, but she still feared being spotted by Michael or Elijah. So, she had worn a ball cap and thick sunglasses all day—probably not the best attire for a potential job candidate.

As she neared the motel, she saw a small, brick building with a sign identifying it as the public library. She smiled. Perhaps looking for online job postings was the way to go!

Lexi headed inside and made her way to the counter to inquire about using a computer terminal. The woman at the counter gave her a friendly smile and asked if she needed help. The name on her tag was Violet. "I was wondering if there's a computer here I can use," Lexi asked.

"Sure. Just sign in, please," Violet said, pushing a faded, sign-in sheet toward her. Lexi started to write her name, but thought better of it. She paused, then signed her name as Laura, just in case there was a possibility of being recognized. "Okay, let me take you to a computer," Violet said, leading Lexi to a terminal located in the back corner by the children's books. "Do you need help with anything in particular on the computer?" Violet asked politely.

Lexi couldn't help but notice the lady was staring at her bruises. "No, I can handle it. Thanks."

Lexi spent nearly an hour searching for online job postings. A few of them seemed promising, but most of them did not. She filled out some online applications and created a résumé to hand out to potential employers—if she ever found any. She printed out several copies and paid for them. As she was leaving, she scanned the local bulletin board for any other potential job leads.

Lexi couldn't help but notice a large, white flier with the words inscribed in bubbly, block letters:

"ROOMMATE WANTED"

The writer was seeking a female roommate to share space in a "grand, three-story, turn of the century home" and claimed that rent would be "very reasonably priced for a single woman's budget." *Sounds too good to be true*, Lexi thought, but she unpinned one of the fliers, folding it into her satchel.

The sunlight was blinding as she stepped out of the library. She pulled out a cigarette and searched her bag for a lighter, coming up empty-handed. She heard the heavy library doors open and close behind her, and then a woman's voice asking, "Do you need a light?"

It was the woman from the counter...Violet or something like that, Lexi remembered.

"Thanks," Lexi replied, leaning forward with her cigarette, inviting the flame and nodding her thanks.

"I couldn't help but notice that you took one of my fliers," Violet said.

At first, Lexi was confused, and actually thought that this woman was accusing her of stealing something. "Oh," she said, feeling foolish as she remembered the flier advertising for a roommate wanted. "Yeah, I did, but I can't get a place right now, anyway. I have to get a job first."

"Are you new in town? I mean...if you don't mind me asking..." Violet asked.

"Yes," Lexi replied, but offered no more information.

"Are you leaving a bad relationship?" Violet asked quietly, again looking over Lexi's bruises with a curious expression.

Lexi was not fond of nosy people, but for some strange reason, she sensed this woman was not like most people. It didn't seem like she was being judgmental, but it did not seem like pity, either. Lexi couldn't put her finger on it, and for the life of her, she could not understand why she would open up to this woman. But she did.

Lexi didn't tell her about Michael or Elijah, but she did tell her about the Clamshell and about that bastard, Reggie. As strange as it was, it felt good to share her woes with this complete stranger.

"Well, I have to go," Lexi told her as she stubbed out her cigarette and gathered her bag on her shoulder. "It was nice talking to you, Violet."

As she started to walk away, Violet called out, "Wait...the address in the flier...why don't you come by tonight? You can check the space out, see if you're interested," she offered.

"Like I told you, I'm looking for work at the moment..." Lexi called back to her.

"Come by anyway," Violet replied. "We'll figure something out."

Chapter Twenty-Eight

Finding Michael was no difficult task. Penelope simply called his secretary again. She knew that if he wasn't home, he was either with his mistress or at work. Michael had a tendency to throw himself into his work whenever he was stressed, and she wasn't surprised when his secretary confirmed that Michael was indeed working today. "He just went to lunch with a business investor, but I expect him back in an hour," Peppy informed her. "Shall I give him a message?"

"No, thank you. I'll catch up with him later," Penelope assured her. And catching up with Michael was exactly what she planned to do.

Penelope had to admit that sitting outside of Michael's work felt slightly stalker-ish, but she loved him and felt compelled to fix things. At the very least, she had to try. Michael was a stickler for punctuality, and at one o'clock precisely, his Jeep Cherokee pulled into the front parking lot. Penelope was waiting for him. Before he could even step out of his vehicle, she was standing there at his side.

Michael closed his eyes, bracing himself for another attack, but she surprised him by throwing her arms around him in a strong embrace.

"I love you," she whispered, holding on to him as long as she could. She searched his eyes questioningly, trying to gauge his reaction.

Michael's eyes were tearful, and his expression was riddled with guilt. He wiped his eyes with the back of his polo sleeve and said, "I never meant to hurt you, Penelope."

"Michael," she began, "I know you've been through a lot when it comes to relationships. I know Lexi broke Elijah's heart and yours when she left. And I know," she continued, "that it's been stressful, planning the wedding, getting a house that you didn't really want…"

He lifted his hand to stop her. "No, there's no excuse for cheating on you. I had no right to do that."

His words resonated in Penelope's heart and for a moment, she was certain that they could recover from this and move forward with the life they had planned. But then she heard the words that would stop her heart for what seemed like forever.

"I think I love her, Penn." Michael buried his face in his hands, unable to look at her. Once upon a time, he had loved Penelope. He had wanted to marry her. She was a great mother, and he had always been able to rely on her. But Violet…

Part of Michael almost wished he'd never run into Violet that night at the bar. He would have been just fine raising his son and stepdaughter with Penelope. They had a happy life together, they really did. Such a thought surprised him, and he looked into the eyes of his fiancée, and for the first time in a long time, he remembered his reasons for asking her to marry him. She was kind and beautiful, and most of all, she loved him and his son unconditionally.

Penelope was stunned by his proclamation, and he immediately wished he could take it back. He reached for her, but she cringed at his touch and stepped back.

"Penelope, wait. I do love you," he pleaded.

"Well, which is it, Michael? Do you love her or me?" she demanded. The length of his silence was unbearable. Penelope threw up her hands and turned to walk away.

"I know you don't owe me any favors, but do you think you could wait?" Michael asked.

"Wait for what?" she asked.

"I have an opportunity to go to Chicago for a business deal. I'll be back in a month. Will you give me some time to sort through my feelings?"

Penelope felt an impulse to slap him just then, but somewhere deep inside, she could still feel a small glimmer of hope—hope that somehow, some way, this could all still be repaired. "Okay," she agreed. "Should we tell the children?"

"No. Let's wait, shall we?" he pleaded.

"I won't tell them," she promised. "I do love Elijah. You know that, right? I never would have abandoned him the way Lexi did."

"I know," he replied.

"At least I'll get to spend one last month with him," she concluded, more to herself than to him.

Penelope turned around and walked back to her car. "Whatever you decide, Michael," she called back to him, "I can live with it." And she could.

Chapter Twenty-Nine

Violet swung her hips from side to side, enjoying the beat of a familiar song. It was one of those catchy songs that radio stations love to play over and over because they never get old. Violet sang along as she twirled through the kitchen with a fresh pan of her famous pecan-crusted salmon. She mixed together butter, honey, pecans, and breadcrumbs, and then lightly spread the glaze on each filet.

Violet felt slightly foolish for making so much food for one person, but in the back of her mind, she was sort of hoping that the girl from the library, Laura, might show up and take her up on her offer to be roommates. She kind of liked the idea of having a roommate, and she knew that Laura needed this too, after hearing her story at the library today. Violet was no stranger to domestic violence, having a sister who had endured similar circumstances to the ones Laura described. Violet also grew up with a father who was a mean drunk, and she knew what it felt like to be afraid and alone. Violet had few, if any, female friends, and perhaps she was being too idealistic, but she enjoyed the idea of a live-in female companion.

Violet slid the pan into the broiler and turned the radio up for her favorite part.

Maybe it was her feelings for Michael, or simply the airy smell of summer drifting in from the screen door, but she felt happy and free. She danced like no one was watching, and she finished the song with a clumsy twirl. She nearly jumped out of her skin as she came face-to-face with someone standing at the screen door.

"Ummm...sorry," Lexi stammered. She burst into a fit of giggles.

Violet did the same. "Well, after that, you might as well come on in," Violet offered, pushing open the screen door for her guest. "How long were you watching me?" she asked, feeling slightly embarrassed.

"I just walked up," Lexi reassured her. "I'm sorry. The door was open, and I was just about to knock on the screen..."

"It's okay. I hope my dance moves didn't scare you away," Violet joked, pulling out a chair to offer a seat.

"Well, I am a professional dancer, you know. I could offer some pointers..." Lexi joked back.

"Tempting," Violet said with a smile and opened the refrigerator to retrieve a drink for her guest. "I'm glad you decided to come, Laura, I really am."

***

Violet made sure her guest liked salmon before

fixing them both a plate. She took a seat next to Lexi, and they both dug into their food. "This is delicious!" Lexi complimented her, and they proceeded to make small talk as they finished their meal. Violet talked about her book series and part-time work at the library, and Lexi shared a few funny stories about the characters she had dealt with at the Clamshell. Lexi had worried that coming here would be awkward, but she felt at ease with this woman, and there was a natural sense of kinship between the two.

"Well, now that I've enticed you with my cooking, let me show you the house so you can see where you would be staying," Violet offered.

Lexi thanked her again for the meal and followed her into an extraordinarily large great room. "It's beautiful," Lexi commented, awe-struck by the size of the place, not to mention its exquisiteness. "Why do you want a roommate when you could have this place all to yourself?" Lexi inquired.

Violet told her about her recent separation from Alex, and explained that although she could afford the expenses on her own, it would be easier with a roommate.

"Like I said, this place is gorgeous, Violet. And I would love to rent from you, but I just don't have any income yet. I mean…who knows? It may take weeks or even months for me to get a job. Wouldn't you be better off finding another roommate that can pay you now instead of waiting around on me?"

"Honestly, I have no one else in mind," Violet answered, "and I was thinking we could try it out, rent-free, for a couple months. If it doesn't work out, or you can't find employment, we'll call it quits. But if you do find something, and do want to stay, you can just start paying on the third month."

It sounded too good to be true. With the way her luck was running, it was hard to believe that Lexi had met such a thoughtful person who was so willing to do her this favor.

"Let me show you to your room," Violet continued, and she led the way to the third floor attic space.

"Wow! This place is spectacular," Lexi marveled as she admired a beautiful, canopied bed in the center of the room. Violet also showed her an adjacent bathroom and a roomy, wardrobe closet that occupied the space. It was such a neat little room, and Lexi absolutely adored it.

"My bedroom and office are on the second floor, as well as a few other bedrooms and a bathroom. If you need extra space for your personal items, feel free to use any of the additional bedrooms. I was thinking we could just share the kitchen and living room spaces on the first floor. We have our own bedrooms and bathrooms, so everywhere else can be sort-of like community areas for either of us to use," Violet suggested.

"Sounds wonderful," Lexi responded. And it did. She felt overwhelmed with excitement about her new living quarters.

"I almost forgot the best part!" Violet exclaimed. "You also have a balcony!" Violet used a small skeleton key to unlock a steel-framed door. It led onto an open balcony inside the turret.

"It's like being inside a tower!" Lexi exclaimed,

looking out onto the town of Oaksdale. "Marvelous!"

"In the old days," Violet explained, "turrets were used to signify military fortification. Soldiers could mount their guns up here, and they were protected from returning fire." Lexi smiled. "I feel safe here."

Violet smiled at her new roommate and potential friend. "Me too," she added thoughtfully.

Chapter Thirty

"Let me help," Penelope offered after observing Michael's uncanny ability to cram everything he owned into a suitcase. Michael stepped aside and watched wordlessly as she refolded his clothes and organized them neatly. *She really is beautiful*, Michael thought, *even when she's doing the most mundane tasks*.

Today he was leaving for Chicago, and possibly leaving behind his relationship with Penelope for good. Michael loved both her and Violet, of this he felt certain. He wasn't sure how running away for a month could solve his dilemma, but he felt that somehow, by removing himself from the situation, a decision would be made.

***

Penelope watched him load his luggage into the Jeep. She remained silent as he hugged his son and kissed her daughter on the cheek. "Goodbye, Sweetheart," he said as he kissed her on the cheek as well.

Penelope watched the man she loved pull away. She could not help but feel as though he was taking her heart with him. She looked at her children and smiled. "Please don't worry," she tried to assure them. "He'll be back before we know it."

***

As Elijah Sinclair watched his father pull away, he was not so sure. He knew his dad well enough to know when something was wrong. "What do you think?" he mumbled quietly to Angie, making sure Penelope was out of hearing range.

Angie sighed. "I think you're right. They really are splitting up," she muttered glumly.

"I have to go to work," Penelope announced. "You two be good."

***

Angela watched her mother pull away after her stepfather. She frowned. Angela liked her stepfather, Michael, and she liked his son even more. She didn't want to lose them.

As though reading her mind, Elijah slipped his hand into hers. "You won't lose me," he promised.

Despite her concerns, Angie believed him, and she somehow knew that some way, she and Elijah would find a way to always stick together.

***

Michael didn't look back as he pulled away from Glenn Heights and headed toward Main Street. The airport was a thirty mile drive from Oaksdale. He still had hours before his flight, but he hated to rush and wanted to give himself plenty of time to check his bags and locate the correct terminal.

As he approached Mandy's Fruit Market, he could almost feel a sense of magnetic allure emanating from the house on the hill. The woman he loved was there, and he wanted nothing more than to see her before he left for Chicago. But he had made a promise to her and to Penelope, so he kept going.

***

Unbeknownst to Michael, Penelope was following him. She had lied to the children about having to work, which was wrong, but she had to know. She had to be certain that Michael was, in fact, going to the airport and not running off for a rendezvous with his mistress. *So far, so good*, Penelope thought, observing that Michael was indeed heading to Interstate 65, which would ultimately take him straight to the airport.

***

Michael was not going to stop at Violet's, but he did slow his speed in hopes of catching a glimpse of her dark hair and incredible blue eyes. *There she is!* he realized excitedly as he noticed her standing on the balcony. God, *she's beautiful*, Michael thought. He would recognize those eyes from a mile away. The woman he loved…the woman…suddenly Michael screeched to a halt, nearly causing the people behind him to wreck, including his fiancée. The woman standing on the balcony was his ex-wife, Lexi Ambrose.

Chapter Thirty-One

When it came to making choices, Lexi's life was riddled with mistakes. But moving in with Violet Cromwell was not one of them. Honestly, Lexi had never felt happier. She loved the house, but that was not all. She and Violet were kindred spirits, and they were growing to be friends as well as roommates.

Lexi did not have many female friends growing up, and she definitely did not make any working in a competitive place like the Clamshell. There was no competition or drama when it came to her and Violet. They just naturally cared for one another and were able to talk to each other like they were family. As days went by, Lexi was becoming more and more confident in her ability to find a job and eventually re-establish some sort of relationship with her son and his father.

Lexi was surprised to learn that her new roommate was a published author, and she eager to receive her assistance in constructing a résumé. They had stayed up late the night before discussing her job options and her vocational skills. Violet offered help, but not the kind that stems from pity. She seemed to truly like Lexi and had a genuine desire to help her get back on her own two feet. Ever since her encounter with Reggie, Lexi had had difficulty sleeping, and had awoken several times in the night screaming for help, begging an unseen phantom to stop hurting her. She and Violet had discussed the symptoms of posttraumatic stress, and Violet had comforted her, sitting quietly by her side until she slipped back into sleep. Violet confided in Lexi about her severed relationship with her husband and admitted that she had been having an affair with another man. Lexi was afraid to tell anyone about Michael or Elijah, but she did tell her nearly everything else. She even told her about the drugs and the unforgettable things she had to do for them. Neither passed judgment on the other, and they got along perfectly like a pair of long lost sisters.

Lexi loved the view from her balcony. She literally felt on top of the world as she appreciated an all-encompassing view of the town of Oaksdale. Michael and Elijah were out there somewhere, and the thought of them was comforting.

A Jeep screeched to a halt on the road below, breaking her trance and interrupting the peaceful quiet of the neighborhood. A man with raven-colored hair and piercing green eyes emerged from the driver's side and cocked his head strangely to look up at her. "Oh, my God!" she gasped. "Michael!" Without a second thought, she raced down the stairs, taking two at a time. She threw open the front door and stared straight into Michael's eyes.

Lexi reached forward to embrace him, but he placed his hands up, as though fending off an attack. "Don't," he said, "what the hell are you doing here, Lexi?"

"I live here now," she explained. "The lady who lives here is renting out some space, and I wanted to be back here in Oaksdale, with you and Elijah."

"With me and Elijah," he repeated, scratching his chin and shaking his head silently.

***

Michael was dumbfounded. Here was this woman, a woman that he loved, a woman who broke his heart when she left him and their young son. He was speechless. Her returning had crossed his mind a million times, but he never actually thought it would happen. In fact, he had given up on that fantasy a long time ago. All he could think to ask was, "Now?"

"I am sorry, Michael. I know I was a piece of shit for leaving. I went to rehab and…well, I'm still working on some things…but I want to see him, Michael. I want to see you."

Michael couldn't believe this. Of all the times for this to happen, it had to happen right now.

"Why, Lexi? Why did you give up on us?" he asked, the pain of losing her all those years ago flooding back in like it had never left.

"I never gave up on my family," she told him. "I just gave up on me."

Michael was still at a loss for words. But finally, the words came to him, and as he spoke, they sounded like they were coming from somebody else. "I forgive you, Lexi."

Lexi reached for him again, but again he pulled back. "That doesn't mean you can see Elijah. And that doesn't mean there can be anything between us. I'm on my way to the airport. I'll be in Chicago for about a month. Get your shit together, and we'll talk when I get back."

"Okay," she agreed.

Michael turned and walked away, still baffled by this most recent encounter. Violet, Penelope, and now Lexi. For a moment, he almost wondered if he was on some demented game show in which the entire premise was to torture him. He got in his Jeep and left the town of Oaksdale.

***

Lexi leaned against the doorframe and took a deep breath. She couldn't believe what had just transpired. She didn't have to go to Michael; Michael had found his way to her. *It is fate*, she decided, and in her heart, she just knew that he would choose to have her back.

Lexi fixed herself a glass of tea and sat down in a rose-backed, kitchen chair. Violet had gone to a meeting with her editor. Lexi felt bad for being less than honest with her new friend and decided that tonight she would tell her everything, including her real reason for coming to Oaksdale.

Chapter Thirty-Two

Penelope watched as Michael pulled away. She didn't follow him this time. "What on God's green earth is going on?" she cried out, throwing her hands up in exasperation.

Last week she had discovered her fiancé in a hotel room with a woman she didn't know, and then tonight she had witnessed an encounter between him and his ex-wife. Nothing made sense to her.

Maybe I'm marrying a complete psychopath, Penelope wondered. *Hell, maybe he is screwing two women behind my back!*

Right on cue, a faded purple Geo Tracker pulled into the driveway of the house, and as the driver emerged, Penelope simply could not believe her eyes. It was, in fact, the other woman from the Filmont Inn, and she was going inside the same house as Michael's ex-wife! *Wow,* Penelope thought, *my fiancé really is a sick, twisted weirdo. He's having some sort of bizarre ménage a trois, involving his ex-wife and one of her friends!*

Penelope was blown away by these recent

developments. She had a million questions running through her mind. Tonight, she was going to get her answers. She put the Escalade into park and made her way on foot up to the house on the hill. She needed to talk to her fiancé's mistress—both of them.

Chapter Thirty-Three

Penelope Pinkerton raised the nine-millimeter, took aim at her target and without hesitation, pulled the trigger. She hit her mark.

"Yes!" she cried out excitedly. Penelope removed her earmuffs and turned to smile at her shooting instructor. "I did it!" she exclaimed, beaming with pride.

"Bull's-eye!" her instructor, Jason Stiffley, announced, pulling her paper target forward for inspection. "I don't think you need an instructor anymore," he said with a lopsided, toothy grin.

"A man like you is always worth keeping around," she said, giving him a flirtatious wink. He seemed to like that comment, and he stepped aside as she brushed past him with her gun case and small ammunition bag in hand.

Shooting was exhilarating for her, and she was still coming down from the rush of adrenaline as she pulled away from the indoor shooting range. She was headed to meet some friends for lunch, which was a good thing because she was absolutely starving. The excitement from her new hobby had left her feeling giddy, and she was ready to share the news of her successful day at the range with her friends.

Penelope found a parking spot and quickly combed her sweaty hair into a high ponytail. Shooting the gun made her feel not only alive, but beautiful. She decided against redoing her makeup and headed into Jay's Diner, walking at a brisk pace. She was disappointed to see that her friends had yet to arrive, but she settled into a corner booth on her own anyway.

A pleasingly plump waitress received her drink order with a smile. For Penelope, the waitress's enthusiasm, which normally would seem facetious or nettlesome, was comforting. *There's nothing wrong or fake about being genuinely polite and cheerful to strangers*, she realized. She didn't want to be a cynic anymore; she didn't want to be like her mother. She only wanted to be happy, and perhaps, she thought, I can just *fake it 'til I make it*. Lately, for some reason, the sun seemed a little brighter and the grass a little greener for Penelope. She wasn't sure why exactly, but she enjoyed having a fresh perspective.

Penelope gave a swift wave as she saw her friends stroll through the diner door. They saw her too, and waved back as they made their way over to where she sat. They slid into the booth opposite of her, and Penelope flashed a subtle smile at Violet Cromwell and Lexi Ambrose.

For an instant, as she looked into the faces of her newfound friends, everything surrounding her seemed hazy and surreal. It was hard to believe that only two short weeks had passed since she had marched up to the house on the hill, determined to have it out with Michael's apparent mistresses.

Penelope rang the doorbell—not once, but six times. When that didn't produce a speedy result, she began banging on Violet's door with a closed fist. "Open up, damn it! We need to have a chat!" she shouted through the door.

***

When Lexi Ambrose opened the door, a look of confusion crossed her pretty face as her eyes rested upon this bewildered woman who was rapping on the door so frantically. The woman looked plumb crazy, but Lexi was used to crazy, so she shrugged and turned back to call for her roommate. "Who the hell…?" Violet asked, stepping forward to identify this unruly caller.

"Close the door, Laura!" Violet bellowed, seemingly recognizing the crazy woman, and she tried to slam the door closed before Lexi even had the chance.

But the woman was determined, and just like they do in the movies, she jammed her foot in the door, preventing it from closing. "Ouch!" she yelped, and instinctually jumped back, reaching down to massage her tender foot.

Instead of closing the door again, Violet opened it wide and apologized. "Are you okay?" she asked tentatively.

"What the hell's that door made of—steel?"

Penelope asked angrily, glaring at her in a classic *if looks could kill* kind of way.

Violet led Penelope, limping, to a kitchen chair, and Lexi went to the refrigerator to fetch ice. Penelope massaged her aching foot and frowned. "I think you broke my toe."

Violet stared down at the foot, horrified, and the three of them were silent. All eyes were on the foot. Lexi snorted softly, breaking the silence, "It's just a toe. She's not going to die. Let's not make this any more dramatic than it already is." She raised her eyebrows at the women.

"What the hell is going on, anyway? Who are you?" Lexi asked, pointing a finger at Penelope. "And why the hell did you slam the door on her like that?" she asked, looking at her roommate curiously.

"I'm sorry," Violet told Penelope. "I just didn't want you to attack me again."

"Again?" Lexi asked, looking back and forth between them.

"You didn't tell her?" Penelope asked, and now it was her turn to laugh.

"She's just my roommate as of recently," Violet explained. "I just met her last week."

"Tell me what?" Lexi asked.

Penelope erupted with laughter again. "Roommates for a week, and you're already sharing men! That's despicable!"

***

"We're not sharing Michael," Violet replied,

sitting down in exasperation. She covered her face with her hands, feeling exhausted by this ludicrous inquisition.

For a moment, time stood still. And then Lexi said quietly, "What about Michael?"

Violet lifted her head from her hands abruptly. "How could you possibly know anything about Michael Sinclair?"

Lexi looked at her roommate, and then to Penelope. She backed up slowly. "Somebody please tell me what's going on."

"And the plot thickens!" Penelope cackled unsteadily, seemingly coming unhinged. "Let me get this straight," she continued, "you..." she said, pointing across the table at Violet, "are screwing my fiancé. And you," she said, pointing at Lexi, "are also screwing him, but neither of you know about it?"

***

Penelope was baffled and was beginning to wonder if she was on one of those candid camera TV shows. This didn't seem so funny anymore. In fact, it never really was. She felt like crying, but she was all cried out. Her marriage to Michael was over, and she could feel it...all the way down to her bones.

"Wait a minute," Lexi said. "I haven't screwed Michael in a long time. In fact, until tonight, I hadn't seen him in nearly a decade."

Violet was shaking her head in disbelief. "Laura, I don't understand—"

"Her name isn't Laura," Penelope announced, laughing again, heartily. "Unless that's the stage name she's going by these days…"

For a moment, it looked as though Lexi might tackle her, but then the look of defeat returned, and she sighed, turning to her roommate. "My name is Lexi. I'm Michael's ex-wife," she explained. She turned to Penelope. "Now, who are you?"

"I'm Michael's fiancé," Penelope muttered, "or at least I was."

"And I guess that just leaves me," Violet said with her head hung low. "I'm the despicable mistress."

***

Minutes passed before anyone spoke again. It was Lexi's voice that broke the silence. "I'm sorry, Violet. I had no idea. And I'm sorry I lied to you about my name. I just didn't want Michael or Elijah to know I was in town yet, but I guess it doesn't matter, because he found me all on his own. I guess…" she wondered thoughtfully, "he was probably looking for you when he rode by the house and saw me on the balcony. Stupid me…I actually thought it was fate calling." Lexi continued to look at her roommate and friend, searching for some sign that she hated her or hopefully a sign that she didn't.

As though reading her mind, Violet said, "I'm not mad at you, Lexi. You didn't know."

"I ditched the plane," Penelope muttered, staring off into the distance.

"What plane?" Violet asked, raising her eyebrows and looking over at Lexi.

"The one Lexi sent Elijah," she explained and turned her eyes to Lexi. "I thought you were the one having an affair with Michael, and I was so distraught…"

"How is he?" Lexi asked, realizing that this stranger was, in fact, an integral part of her son's life.

Penelope blurted out, "He's a terrific kid."

"Thank you for helping to take care of him," Lexi said, and slowly pulled out a chair so that she could join the other two women at the table. "I've had some pretty weird days in my life, but this one takes the cake."

"Agreed," Violet said, still shaking her head in disbelief.

"You know," Penelope said, "we may be in opposition to one another, but we do have one thing in common, and that's Michael Sinclair."

The women stared at each other, and for a brief moment, they all felt an unexpected sense of camaraderie. Violet stood to make coffee, but thought better of it, and headed for the liquor cabinet. "Anyone care for a drink?"

Over drinks, they all came to the same conclusion. Michael would be back in a month, and he would then make his choice between them. They all loved him, and although that put them at odds, in a strange way, it was exactly what brought them together.

The women talked for hours. Perhaps it was the liquor flowing through their bloodstreams or maybe something else, but the conversation came easily and was not confrontational. Lexi was candid about her marriage to Michael, and she admitted that her choices had been poor. Despite Penelope's knowledge about Lexi's past misdeeds, she could not help but like the woman. She had a quirky demeanor, and she was funny—in a dark and cynical way—as was she. Lexi explained that she honestly had no idea who either of them were until today, and as she realized Penelope's role as stepmother to Elijah, she began to ask more and more questions about him. As a mother herself, Penelope understood this mother's love for her child and her yearning to learn more about him.

Penelope learned that Violet, on the other hand, was well aware of her and Michael's engagement, and although she should have hated her for having an affair with him, it was not Violet who had pledged to marry her and remain faithful; it was Michael who betrayed her, not Violet, nor his ex-wife. She was beginning to see that they all loved him in their very own individual ways, and for some reason, this made her feel closer to these women; they understood the allure of Michael's charm, and they all wondered what it would feel like if they lost him.

After hours of conversation and multiple cocktails, Penelope was too intoxicated to drive home. She asked for a phone book to locate a cab service, but Violet and Lexi insisted she stay. She was too exhausted and drunk to refuse the offer, and she passed out promptly under a wooly afghan on the couch in Violet's great room.

The evening had been so unexpected and bizarre, but it would not be their last evening together. They met for dinner and drinks later that same week, and as hard as it was to believe, they did not once mutter his name; instead, they spoke of other topics; Lexi's crazy stories about the Clamshell, Violet's brilliant new series—which strangely enough, Penelope had read—and Penelope spoke of her daughter and Elijah.

***

Lexi stayed quiet during these moments as though she were trying to take it all in and hold on to the information as long as possible. The women were all so different; their appearances, their professions, and even their values; yet, somehow, they found some sort of common ground, and perhaps their contrasting personalities complimented each other's.

And now here we are today, sitting in a diner like we have been friends for years, Penelope thought, incredulously. It was a strange thought indeed. Since their first encounter, the three women had met for lunch on three separate occasions. Oddly enough, with the exception of the first night, they still never discussed the elephant in the room: Michael.

"So, how did it go at the shooting range?" Violet asked, interrupting Penelope's line of thought.

"Yeah," Lexi chirped in, "did Stiffley get a stiffy over your shooting skills?" she joked.

Penelope chuckled. "He is pretty handsome, I

must admit, but not as handsome as…" she did not finish the sentence. She didn't have to. "And in fact," she said instead, "I actually hit the bull's-eye today!"

"Impressive!" Violet cheered, clapping her hands together. "Remind me never to piss you off." Violet then paused, realizing how silly she sounded. She had, in fact, pissed off Penelope Pinkerton on a couple of occasions. And with that said, all three women burst into a fit of giggles.

They were such an odd pairing, really, but somehow, it made sense among them. The waitress returned for their food orders, and each woman ordered a different dish: a light chicken salad for Penelope, a hamburger for Lexi, and a ribeye for Violet.

After paying their bill, they stepped out of Jay's Diner only to be met with a torrential downpour. They found a roomy space under the dusty grey awning, and Violet and Lexi lit cigarettes.

"You don't mind, do you?" Violet asked Penelope, using her hand to waft the pungent smoke in an opposite direction.

"Nah…I used to smoke, but I gave it up," Penelope revealed with a shrug. "I used to love it…smoking, I mean…and sometimes it's still hard to believe that I don't. Sometimes the things you love the most are also the things that hurt you. And once you give them up, living without them seems impossible. But after a while…you just do," Penelope said softly, and her words hung in the air as all three women stood there, silently huddled together against the rain.

"We should all quit," Lexi said, and for an instant, perhaps they all realized they were no longer talking about cigarettes.

"Okay," Violet broke in, "I have an idea I want to run by you, Lexi. And just hear me out..." Lexi raised her eyebrows. "So, I was thinking maybe you could put some of your stripper skills to good use."

Lexi frowned.

"Wait. You said you were going to hear me out," Violet whined.

"Okay, I'm listening," Lexi said, chuckling at her friend's persistence.

"So, what if you offered a stripper class for the women in this town?" Penelope snorted, and Lexi continued to frown. "I'm serious!" Violet said.

"I seriously doubt there are any aspiring strippers in this town," Lexi pointed out.

"No, no, that's not what I meant," Violet assured her. "I'm talking about doing some sort of stripper-cise class instead of aerobics or going to the gym. The idea of it may be a little unorthodox around here, but that is exactly why I think people will come check it out to begin with. I'm not trying to undermine your other skills, Lexi, I just think that you should try to capitalize on your athleticism and dancing abilities. The other night you told me that even as a young girl you loved to dance."

"I would join a class like that," Penelope spoke up, "if dancing like a stripper could make me have a body like yours. I would be willing to pay big bucks to join that club. Plus, I think it would be sort of fun—more fun than lifting weights or doing crunches."

Lexi remained wordless, and she was chewing on her bottom lip.

Violet instantly looked regretful. "Lexi…"

"I love it!" Lexi squealed, reaching for her roommate and pulling her into a tight hug.

She pulled back. "But I don't even have a building space to start up something like this…" Lexi said.

"I've already thought of that," Violet said, wrapping an arm around her friend and flashing her brightest smile. "We'll just use some of the unused space in my house! We can really make this work, Lexi!" The three of them squealed with joy at the plan for Lexi's new business venture.

The excitement of the moment was interrupted by the sound of Penelope's cell phone ringing. Violet continued to rattle on about all of their grand plans, but Lexi did not take her eyes off of Penelope.

Penelope's face was ashen.

"What is it?" Violet asked, coming over to stand beside her.

"It's Elijah. He was riding home with one of his school friends, and there was an accident. He's at the hospital," Penelope explained breathlessly. Penelope was trembling. She started to dig frantically for her keys, but Lexi was already running toward Violet's Tracker. Violet and Penelope ran after her. Violet climbed in behind the wheel, and the other women climbed in through the passenger door.

"Lexi, I thought we agreed that you would wait to talk to Michael before trying to see Elijah,"

Penelope said gently.

"Well, Michael's not here for me to ask, now, is he?" Lexi snapped. "You're his stepmother, and I'm going with you to make sure our son is okay," she said, and she squeezed Penelope's hand tightly in her own.

Chapter Thirty-Four

Violet was not a religious woman, but she closed her eyes and said a prayer anyway as she watched her two friends run through the double glass doors of Morton University Hospital. She did not go in. She had no reason to. She may have loved Michael, but his son was a stranger to her, and she had no business intruding at a time like this. She leaned against the brick side of the building. She would wait all night if she had to. She needed to know that this young man, who was so important to her friends and to Michael, was alive and well.

***

The first thing Penelope saw as she threw open the emergency room doors was her daughter pacing the floor in front of a hospital room. She ran to meet her and held her in an embrace. "He's okay, Mom," Angela whispered into her mother's hair as she clutched her. Those words felt like a giant boulder being lifted from her palpitating heart.

157

She nodded to Lexi. "He's okay," she told her. Lexi collapsed to her knees. Angela looked at this woman, and then to her mother inquisitively, but there was no time for explanations. "We need to see him," she said breathlessly, and she and Lexi slipped into the room hurriedly.

Elijah was sleeping peacefully. "It's just the painkillers," a nurse explained to them. "All he has is a broken collar bone. He's one of the lucky ones. The medicine knocked him out cold, though," she said and left them to be with their son.

His eyes fluttered, and the first words out of his mouth were, "Mom?" Neither woman moved, but then his eyes locked onto Penelope, and she rushed to be at his side. "I'm so glad you're okay," she said, and she stroked his cheek tenderly.

***

Elijah looked down at the IV in his arm and then around the hospital room as though he were just now realizing what happened. His eyes passed over the dark-haired beauty in the doorway then stopped and returned to her again.

Lexi had imagined this moment so many times— him seeing her after all these years, and although she had dreamed of several different outcomes, she did not expect what happened next.

Her beautiful, softhearted, wise beyond his years son smiled brightly and reached out for her. Lexi didn't hesitate. She ran to her son and held him like she might never let go. And this time around, she most certainly would not.

Chapter Thirty-Five

Michael Sinclair felt like the luckiest man in the world. The fact that his luggage was the first to emerge from the chute on the baggage carousel seemed to confirm it. He grabbed his suitcase and left the airport, making his way to the space where his Jeep Cherokee was parked.

Michael could not believe that an entire month had passed since his dramatic departure from Oaksdale. When he left, he'd been dazed and confused by his romantic options. He was engaged to Penelope, who would make a superb wife and mother for any man, but then there was Violet, the young girl that he obsessed over as a youth; their passion was intense and fiery. Lastly, there was Lexi: his first true love and mother to his only son. He arrived in Chicago completely befuddled, and he had stayed that way until three short days ago when it all became crystal clear...

Michael had gone to Chicago for business, and that's exactly what his trip consisted of: conference calls, board meetings, and lots of meaningless hand shaking. Perhaps if he were being honest with himself, he might admit that he relished having such a nonstop schedule, as it permitted him to avoid making a decision about whom he truly loved.

On his third to last day, his business was complete and, therefore, all distractions ceased, leaving him alone in a big city with an even bigger decision to make. He had opted to go sightseeing, which was totally out of character for him, but he enjoyed himself immensely that day. The day was absent of pressure and filled with faceless strangers, making him feel at ease for the first time in weeks.

He took a stroll through Wrigley Field, and he marveled at some exquisite works of art at the art and history museum. At the end of the day, he perched on the sky deck of the Willis Tower, and it was then that he knew. There was only one woman he wanted beside him.

Michael rolled down his windows and hummed along to a familiar tune as he coasted along Interstate 65. He could not wait to see her.

Michael was not happy about having to break the hearts of two others, but he was flying on cloud nine as he pushed the pedal harder, hurtling toward the woman of his dreams and ultimately their future together. He was excited to see her face when he told her, and all he wanted was to hold her close in his arms.

Chapter Thirty-Six

Today was the day Michael was supposed to meet Violet at the Filmont Inn, and as he made a sharp turn from Main Street, he was right on time. He jogged through the front entrance and addressed the young, freckled girl who was stationed at the front desk.

"A reservation for Violet Cromwell, please…or maybe…" Michael scratched his chin, "…it might be under my name, Michael Sinclair." The girl barely glanced up from her iPhone, but she did hand him a key card. Room 206, how could he forget?

Michael took his time getting to the room, opting to take the stairs. He let out a deep breath, slid the card through the key reader, and stepped into the familiar room.

He was surprised to see that the beds were still made in a fashion one can only attribute to a seasoned maid service staff. Violet wasn't there, and initially, he thought perchance she had yet to arrive, but then he noticed a cream-colored sheet of paper on the bed. He sat down to read her letter.

Dear Michael,

I have loved you since I was a little girl, but I am no longer a girl. When we are young, we live by the seat of our pants, and that makes life exciting, but as adults we must be resolute in our decisions, and I am resolute in mine. Our ship has sailed, Michael. There are two other beautiful women who love you, and I hope you make the right choice. You know how you rescued me that day when I was eleven? Well, my dear Michael, you rescued me again from a marriage that I did not belong in, from a life that was not mine. And for that, I will be forever grateful. I leave you with a brilliant quote from Robert James Waller:

"The old dreams were good dreams; they didn't work out, but I'm glad I had them."

Love always, Violet

There is something so uncanny about returning home after a long vacation. For a split second, everything inside your house seems unfamiliar and strange, and you may notice little things that you take for granted or fail to notice on a day-to-day basis. Time apart can do that; it makes you readjust your outlook from a different angle.

Michael experienced this exact feeling when he opened the front door of his and Penelope's new home in Glenn Heights. Although he originally despised the cookie cutter design, he had to admit that it was genuinely stunning, and he admired Penelope's ability to make the space look clean and sterile, but also homey and inviting. As he looked around at the pictures and decorations she had added, he noted her superb attention to detail. The house smelled so good; it was a familiar scent that he hadn't noticed before—at least not consciously. God he missed her, and he missed this place they called their home.

The kids were in school and Penelope was not home, so he walked slowly around the empty space, enjoying the memories and avoiding the letter on the table. Her engagement ring was beside it, and he didn't need to read it to know what it said, but he felt compelled to read her words.

Dear Michael,

I loved you. I still love you.

But I love myself more.

I deserve to be with someone who KNOWS that they want to be with me, and you deserve to be happy. Penelope

Michael's eyes were so blurry with tears that he nearly missed her where she stood beside his Jeep—

not Penelope but Lexi. "What are you doing here?" he asked, his voice cracking.

"Penelope told me when your flight was landing, and I know she went to work, so I was hoping to catch you here, in person," Lexi said, and she reached up to wipe a tear from his face. "I want you to know that I'm sorry for leaving you and Elijah, and I know it will never be enough..." Michael began to speak, but she shushed him. "Please, Michael, I need to say this...sometimes I don't think I was cut out for motherhood. I learned right away that taking care of a child requires a type of selflessness that I never saw in my own parents and never quite mastered myself. I didn't think I could do it, so I ran like a coward. I used men and drugs to mask the pain: the pain of my childhood, the pain of my life in general. I can never take back what I did, but coming back here made me realize something...Elijah turned out just fine without me, just as I did, in spite of my own crappy upbringing. We are fighters, he and I. He's a wonderful young man, and that's to your credit, Michael. You made up for what I was lacking, and you did what I couldn't, and I will love you forever because of that. I can't change what has happened, but I can make changes right now, at this moment. Instead of focusing on trying to fix what we had, or create a love life for myself, I am going to do one thing, and one thing only, and that is focus on the most important man that ever walked into my life, and that is Elijah."

Michael squeezed her tightly, and then watched her climb behind the wheel of the old, run-down

Malibu. No longer did she resemble that helpless, homeless girl at the bus station in Reno. She was older now, and the weight of the world and her burdensome life were etched in the creases on her forehead and showed in her gait. Despite the fact that she looked older, there was an elegance in her step, and she had never seemed more exquisite to him. He would miss her, but he had grown accustomed to missing Lexi.

Chapter Thirty-Seven

When her doorbell chimed, Violet anticipated a variety of possible visitors, but she was unprepared for the stranger on her doorstep. "I'm Lucas Middleton, and I used to live in this house," he blurted out nervously. "I know this is a bizarre request, but I was hoping I could come inside...maybe look around and sort of say goodbye."

Allowing a stranger into her home was definitely a big no-no in Violet's book, but she opened her door for him anyway. It was a strange request, but somehow nothing seemed all that strange to Violet anymore these days. Violet and Lucas walked through the kitchen and down the corridor silently, and she observed as he examined the changes she had made to the house and seemingly took it all in.

"I had a stupid argument with my father," he said abruptly. "I left for college the next day, and I never looked back...he was a difficult man, my father," he continued, "but I sure did love him. I drove all the way from Arizona to visit his grave. I wish I would have come sooner, before my father…you know, died," he said, swallowing down the lump in his throat. "I'm sorry for just showing up, but I wanted to see the house one last time."

Lucas shook her hand and headed for the door. Violet hesitated but then asked, "Would you like to stay for dinner?" She wasn't sure why, but she liked this man, and the pain in his eyes was very real and somehow seemed endearing. She lit the gas stove and began cooking as he watched her from his seat at the table.

Violet did not know what the future held for her. Perhaps there would be many men and many moments just like this before she found the right one. Perhaps her search had nothing to do with love and more to do with finding her true self and learning how she fit into this world. As for now, she was content with not knowing and determined to just live in the moment.

Chapter Thirty-Eight

"I told you I was good for it," Lexi teased, holding out a wad of cash for her mechanic. The Malibu had a new tire and a tune-up, and she was ready to hit the open road. She and Elijah had flown back to her old town to pick up the Malibu, and they planned to drive it back to Oaksdale following the scenic route in order to spend more quality time together.

Elijah had recently obtained his drivers' permit, and he was surprised when his mother tossed him the keys. "I don't know, Mom," he said apprehensively.

"Come on, let me teach you something," she pleaded, and he smiled, sliding into the driver's seat. "Before we leave town, I need you to make one stop," Lexi told him. She gave him directions to her old apartment building and asked him to wait in the car.

Lexi knocked on her ex-neighbor's door and was taken aback by the gorgeous hottie who opened it. He appeared to be in his early thirties with dark brown hair and greenish-gray eyes. "Are you Danny?" she inquired. When he confirmed who he was, she thanked him for saving her life.

"I'm only sorry I didn't do something sooner," Danny said, scratching his head sheepishly.

"Me too," she said.

Danny opened the door wider. "Do you want to come in?" He seemed so handsome at first, but as she looked closer with her new, more perceptible eyes, she saw that he was tall and gangly, and the creases of his arms were marked with small, purplish patches. Lexi knew he'd saved her life and she should be kind, but she knew his type, and would run from the likes of any man that resembled him. "Come on, just for a minute," he said, waving her in with a similarly patchy hand. "Why don't you make it up to me for saving your life and all…" His eyes moved up and down the contours of her body, his tongue lolling out the side of his mouth.

"Sure," Lexi said, quietly pulling a card from her pocket. "This is the name of a place where you can go to get help. The number is on the back. If you really want, I'll drive you there now. It's not far from here. I went there once, and it saved my life, and I would love an opportunity to return the favor." He slapped at the card angrily, and Lexi left him to his misery but not before sliding the card through the slot in his door.

Lexi jogged down the steps and was relieved to feel her shoes hit the asphalt. Elijah was waiting for her, but he was no longer in the driver's seat. He looked so handsome sitting there in the old Malibu, his legs tucked up under him in the seat; he had sat that way since he was six; his posture was endearing, and it melted Lexi's heart. She imagined him sitting close to the radiator in the run-down apartment near campus, doing his best to stay warm, as he looked at a picture book all by himself—the one that she bought but never once read to him; he just sat there, quiet as a mouse, as she lay strung out on the sofa bed, watching him, unable to move.

His forgiveness was a blessing for Lexi, and she would never stop trying to make it up to him. Thinking of her past mistakes no longer triggered much guilt; her past was now a reminder of how far she had come, and she knew that her relationship with Elijah would only grow stronger. "So, you don't want to drive, eh?" she asked, raising her eyebrows at him curiously.

"Nah. I just want to enjoy the ride for a while. I want to enjoy this moment with you."

Elijah Sinclair looked at his mother, and he felt proud of her. He had always loved her, and despite her faults as a mother, his early memories of her were mostly good. He was only happy to have her back in his life.

Chapter Thirty-Nine

Coach Elly Anderson saw Penelope approaching, and she braced herself for another lecture on why Angela should not be in the back of the formation. She was surprised to note that Penelope seemed to be smiling, and she was carrying what appeared to be a small gift in her palm.

"Angela picked this out for you," she offered, handing her a tiny box.

The coach opened it to discover a small charm of a darling little girl with pompoms in her hands raising her arms in a V.

"I'm not trying to butter you up so you'll make Angie captain," Penelope assured her with a clever smirk.

"Well, I wasn't going to say that, but I was wondering..." Coach Anderson admitted, a low chuckle emitting from her chest.

"I just wanted to say I'm sorry for acting like a royal pain. You are a terrific coach, and I have realized that it doesn't matter where Angie stands within the squad; her smile and personality will shine through. Angie has been incredibly happy since she came to Riverside and joined your team, so I just want to thank you for that."

Elly smiled and thanked her for the gift.

"Did you give her the charm?" Angela called out, running over to where her mother and coach stood near the sidelines of the basketball court.

"Yes, she did! Thank you, Sweetheart!" Elly exclaimed, patting Angie on the shoulder.

"I want you to know that I have decided that when I grow up, I want to be a coach like you," Angie announced. Angie looked at her mother to gauge her reaction, concerned that the idea of becoming a coach might seem silly and unimportant to her. But Penelope was smiling, and she had never felt more proud of her daughter.

Mother and daughter headed out of the gym; they walked arm in arm, just like they always had. As they got into the car, Penelope felt an overwhelming sense of sadness as she searched the rearview mirror for Elijah's face, and he was no longer there. "I miss him," Penelope said, and there was no need to explain, because Angie missed him too. Penelope and Angie had moved into their own flat now, and Elijah was still with his father.

"Well, I have good news and bad news," Angela said. "Which do you want first?"

Penelope rolled her eyes at her daughter's dramatics, and said, "I always like to hear the good news first."

"Okay. Well, even though Elijah does not live with us anymore, you'll be seeing him quite often very soon. And the bad news," she continued, "is that even though I'm not supposed to date, I have agreed to go to the prom with my new, steady boyfriend."

Despite Angie and Elijah's belief that their parents were clueless when it came to teenagers, Penelope already knew what she was going to say. She smiled at her daughter. "I haven't even told you who he is yet!" Angie whined, scowling at her mother.

"I bet I can guess on the first try," Penelope said slyly, and she patted her daughter on the knee lovingly.

Chapter Forty

"I cannot believe you turned that hunk down!" Violet exclaimed, shaking her head after hearing Penelope tell the story of how she turned down her shooting instructor when asked on a date.

"I told him that I'm focusing on me and Angie right now, and I am," Penelope said proudly.

"Wow! I think we're all turning a new leaf," Lexi commented, thinking of how she had walked away from a hunk of her very own. "Speaking of Angie..." Lexi continued, "Do you know...?" she asked Penelope.

Penelope smiled, "About your son asking my daughter to prom?"

"Yes," Lexi said. "How do you feel about it?"

"I think it's perfect," Penelope said, and Lexi nodded in agreement.

"And speaking of perfection..." Violet chimed in, "I saw your turn-out for the stripper-cise class. It was a real hit!"

Lexi smiled. "Thanks for being my inspiration for it. Both of you," she said, smiling at her two best friends. As she looked at them, Lexi could not help but think that having friends like these could trump having love any day of the week.

The three friends were sitting together in a local nightclub, and the night was still young. Lexi lifted her champagne glass. "Let's do a toast!"

They all raised their glasses. "To Elijah and Angie," Violet said. "And to us," Lexi added.

"And," Penelope said, "to every woman I ever scorned in my senseless pursuit of a man."

"Let's dance!" Violet called out, already making her way to the middle of the dance floor. Lexi and Penelope followed behind. "Wait," Lexi stopped her, "do you ever wonder who it was?"

"Who what was?" Penelope called out over the deafening sound of the amplifiers.

"Who Michael would have chosen," Lexi said.

"Nah. Doesn't matter."

Epilogue

Five years later...

The steps of the church were littered with paper confetti and rice. The bride and groom were long gone, but the memory of their extraordinary departure on this blissful day would be eternally etched in the mind of Lexi Ambrose. The ceremony was breathtaking, and Lexi had never felt so content, not in all of the years of her troublesome life. Today her son was married, and seeing him filled with such happiness in turn filled her with an overwhelming sense of satisfaction. She leaned against the hood of her new Volkswagen Beetle, taking in the scene one last time before heading to her eight o'clock class.

"One of the most difficult aspects about leaving Michael was the realization that I would have to give up Elijah as my son," Penelope said, looking at her friend and feeling a similar sense of joy.

"Somehow, some way, fate has a way of correcting itself, because I finally have him back, as my son, and I am so happy for both of our children."

Penelope Pinkerton was thrilled about her daughter's decision to marry Elijah. The young couple had stayed together all of these years despite their attendance to separate colleges and years of long distance correspondence. Elijah had pursued a business degree, following in the footsteps of his father at B & J Shipping, whereas Angela had obtained her teaching certificate, and she was teaching English and assisting Coach Elly Anderson with the Riverside cheerleading squad. "Just think," Penelope said to Lexi, "if you had not come back, if you had just given up, you would not be enjoying this moment right now."

"I know," Lexi replied. "I am so fortunate to have such a forgiving son. And," she added, "I am extremely blessed to have such an exquisite daughter-in-law." The two friends embraced, savoring the final moments of this unforgettable day before heading their separate ways.

"Congrats, ladies!" Violet Cromwell declared, approaching her two best friends. Her soon-to-be-husband, Lucas Middleton, was by her side, and he shook the two ladies' hands amicably. They could not help remarking how radiant Violet looked, with her round, swollen belly and puffy, red cheeks. Lucas and Violet's baby girl was due any day now, and it was obvious that she felt uncomfortable as she attempted to shift the weight on her feet. "I don't know how you guys did it. Being pregnant is miserable!" she complained, chuckling softly.

"All of the pain and discomfort will seem

worthwhile when you are holding your daughter tight in your arms," Penelope assured her.

Lexi thought about the day Elijah was born; she recalled how it felt holding him, and then she recalled how she felt during the time they were apart. "Never let her go," she told Violet softly.

"I won't," Violet said, and she looked at her friend knowingly. The three of them were so close now that they barely had to talk to each other; a simple look or gesture could speak volumes among these friends. They had an unbreakable connection, and their bond was stronger than steel.

"Well, I have to get going. My class starts in a half hour, and I must change out of these clothes," Lexi told them.

There was another round of hugging, and then she got into her new car and pulled away from the church. "She's doing so well," Violet said. She smiled as Lexi's Beetle descended the hill.

"I agree! Her business is flourishing, and she's happier than I have ever seen her," Penelope concurred.

"I think we are too," Violet said, grinning at her friend.

Penelope had to agree. Not only were the children happy, but all of the women were pleased with the current state of their lives. Violet had Lucas and a daughter on the way. By a stroke of fate, Lucas had returned to his childhood home, the place of his childhood recollections, and instead of being met by the haunting memories, he was instead introduced to the woman of his dreams. In some small way, the love he was building with Violet made up for the love he waited too long to build with his father. Violet's panic attacks were few and far between, and her novels were so good that the local bookstores simply could not keep them stocked on the shelves.

Penelope was dating, but mostly she was focusing on herself in a way she had not done since before meeting her first husband. Losing Brian was one of the most painful moments in her life, and leaving Michael was tough. For nearly a year, she had felt lost, and at times, depressed. If it was not for her two best friends, she never would have made it through.

Violet and Lucas said their goodbyes to Penelope, and she was left on her own, staring at the grand, aging church. She had planned to marry Michael here in this very same church, and the memory seemed distant, an idea long forgotten. As she placed her bag of items in the backseat, she noticed one solitary car in the parking lot. It was hard to believe that merely an hour earlier, the lot had been filled to its maximum capacity. As she climbed behind the wheel, she heard the shrill creak of the church door, and she watched as her ex-fiancé trotted down the stone stairway, taking two steps at a time. She could have simply pulled away, but she waited for his approach, and then congratulated him on his son's marriage.

Their son and daughter were married now, and it was inevitable that their paths were going to cross, at least occasionally. Michael saw her waiting for him, and he started to jog toward her eagerly.

He came to a halt beside her window, unsure

now of what he would say.

"Thank you," she spoke first to him, smiling at his awkwardness. "The wedding was beautiful, and I want to thank you, Michael, for what you did today. Walking Angie down the aisle was such a kind act, and although I know she wishes her father could be here on the day of her wedding, I know that she is grateful for you. Even though you never became her stepfather in a literal sense, you played an important role in her life and were the closest thing she has ever had to a father since Brian died."

Her words were so thoughtful, and without thinking, Michael leaned into her and placed his lips on hers. She was startled by his suddenness, and she slapped him harder than she intended.

Stunned, he placed a hand on his cheek, and then grinned sheepishly. "I'm sorry, Penn. I don't know what came over me."

"It's okay," she said, touching her lips, still confused by the kiss.

"I have missed you," he explained, "and I need you to know that I'm sorry for hurting you. I've never had an opportunity to really say that, and I'm sorry that I haven't tried harder to apologize to you."

"It's okay, Michael," she assured him. "I'm over it now. What is meant to happen will happen, and I now know that you and I were not meant to be. I forgave you years ago."

"Thank you," he replied.

Time seemed to stand still for a moment. But then she started the SUV and told him goodbye.

"Wait," he called out before she had a chance to

pull away, "I want you to know that it was you," he said. "That day in Chicago when I stood on the deck of the Willis Tower, it felt like I could see the whole world, and its greatness made me feel on top of the world, literally, and all I could think was how I wanted to share it with you and our children. There was no doubt in my mind that you were the one, and I came home as fast as I could to tell you. All that time, searching for something to fill some void…and that something was right there all along, right under my nose. You were that something, Penelope, and I am a fool for not seeing it sooner."

There was once a time when his words would have brought Penelope to tears, but those days were long gone. "It is too late, Michael. I'm sorry. Right around the same time you were realizing that you loved me, I think I was realizing that I no longer loved you. I will always care for you, Michael, but we cannot erase the past. Thank you for walking my daughter down the aisle. And thank you for leading me here—to this very moment in life, which is right where I'm supposed to be."

Penelope headed home to her new flat. It was not the grand home that she imagined in the dreams of her youth, but she loved it, and she loved being on her own. Hearing Michael say that she was the one he would have chosen should have given her a sense of satisfaction, and at one point in her life, it probably would have. But she no longer drew satisfaction from the misfortunes of others, especially not her closest allies. She would never tell them the truth; there was no need. Their relationship was not one of competition; they relished in each other's achievements, and they rallied together to support each other's losses.

As a girl, Penelope loved nothing more than to tell stories that were all about love: fairy princesses falling in love and living happily ever after with princes. But the real beauty of her life story was not about love—at least not the kind of love shared between women and men. Her story was one of friendship, perseverance, and courage. She had grown as a mother and person, and although her story was not about love, it was filled with an abundance of it. As a child, she naïvely believed that her happiness was dependent on finding love, and the truth be told, she was right. But sometimes love comes in the form of a bond with a friend, sister, teacher, or even one's self. Penelope loved her friends, and she would not trade them for any man in the world. She loved her daughter and her career, and most importantly…she loved herself.

Author's Note and Acknowledgments

All of my books are personal, in one way or another. But this book holds a special place in my heart because it is the first book I ever wrote. It's not perfect. In fact, the very first version was a total wreck. But I wrote it during a hard time in my life and in its own way, this book helped save me. It also helped me discover my love for writing. I never planned on trying to get it published until a year later when I let my sister read it and she pressured me into submitting it to publishers. I was really embarrassed about it at the time, but I want to thank you, Vicki, for always pushing me to believe in myself and take chances, even when I don't want to.

Thank you to the original publisher of this book—Sarah Book Publishing. And thank you to Limitless Publishing, for letting me re-release *This Is Not About Love* into the world.

Thank you to my husband and children for standing by me and for being my only fans in the beginning of this crazy writing journey.

Thank you to my daughter and late grandmother, both named Violet, for letting me borrow your name.

Thank you to my editor, Toni Rakestraw. You work magic on my manuscripts—seriously, I don't know how you do it but I'm so grateful for your help.

Thank you to Deranged Doctor Design for creating this cover.

And a big thank you to all my readers—when the first edition of *This Is Not About Love* was released, I had ZERO readers (besides my family). I'm grateful to each and every one of you for reading my books.

About the Author

Carissa Ann Lynch is the *USA Today* bestselling and award-winning author of the *Flocksdale Files* trilogy, *Horror High* series, *Searching for Sullivan, 13, 13: Deja Vu, Grayson's Ridge, Shattered Time, Things Only the Darkness Knows, Midnight Moss, Twist Me, Twisted, Dark Legends, Shades and Shadows*, and *This Is Not About Love*. She resides in Floyds Knobs, Indiana with her husband, children, and collection of books. Besides her family, her greatest love in life is books. Reading them, writing them, holding them, smelling them…well, you get the idea. She's always loved to read and never considered herself a "writer" until a few years ago when she couldn't find a book to read and decided to try writing her own story. She's a self-proclaimed genre hopper, always experimenting with her craft, and pushing herself to the limits. With a background in psychology, she's always been a little obsessed with the darker areas of the mind and social problems.

Read More from Carissa Ann Lynch

Facebook:
https://www.facebook.com/CarissaAnnLynchauthor

Twitter:
https://twitter.com/carissaannlynch

Amazon Author Page:
http://www.amazon.com/Carissa-Lynch/e/B00REPXXW6/

Website:
https://carissaannlynch.com

Join Carissa's mailing list:
http://eepurl.com/chb46z

www.ingramcontent.com/pod-product-compliance
Lightning Source LLC
Chambersburg PA
CBHW020908180626
46816CB00007BA/2306